COELHO NETO

THE SPHINX

(for Jose Martins Fontes)

Translated by

Shawn Garrett

THIS IS A

STRANGE PORTS PRESS BOOK

ISBN: 979-8-9876810-6-0 (softcover)

ISBN: 979-8-9876810-7-7 (hardcover)

The Translator dedicates this book to his longtime good friend Prof. Pete Groff, whose excellent humor, boundless wisdom and moral counsel have made me a better man for a majority of my life. Thanks man, I wish you were my brother.

As always, all this work is also dedicated to my late, beloved sister Susan M. Garrett.

A MESSAGE OF SOME WARNING

Given the age of some of these narratives, it should not be surprising that occasionally they contain details of character, plot or opinion that express beliefs and prejudices which contemporary society now frowns upon and register as insulting, reductive and counter to the aims of an inclusive society.

Being that, for many (if not all) of these works, this will be their first appearance in English and

1. Trusting to our reader's rational, empathic natures as well as their understanding of the subtleties of history and privilege (in all its facets, both positive and negative)
2. Presuming our readers respect the importance of retaining the entire truth of creative texts as written, "warts and all" as they say
3. We have chosen to leave this material in the text, unchanged, for you to apply your own judgments.
4. The inclusion of these instances should NOT be taken, in any way, as advocacy or support of these unfortunate or hurtful beliefs by STRANGE PORTS PRESS, its staff or any corporate entity associated with it.

TABLE OF CONTENTS

ABOUT THE AUTHOR

COELHO NETO (1864-1934) was born Henrique Maximiano Coelho Neto in the city of Caxias, Maranhão. He was Brazilian writer and politician, who founded and occupied the second chair of the Brazilian Academy Of Letters from 1897 until his death in 1934 and was also its president in 1926. After abandoning his legal studies in 1885, he became part of a group of bohemians, the history of which he wrote in his novels **A CONQUISTO (1899)** and **FOGO FÁTUO (1929)**. He was also a practitioner of the Afro-Brazilian martial art of capoeira and on August 6, 1888, at a speech by Quinto Bocaiuva, he disarmed an attack by hitmen led by an infamous street capoeirista Benjamim. In 1890, he married Maria Gabriela Brandão, daughter of educator Alberto Olympio Brandão, and they had 14 children. He wrote under numerous pseudonyms, including Anselmo Ribas, Caliban, Ariel, Amador Santelmo, Blanco Canabarro, Charles Rouget, Democ, N. Puck, Tartarin, Fur-Fur and Manés. He was active in virtually all literary genres and was for many years the most widely read writer in Brazil, however, he and his work were attacked by the Modernists during the Semana de Arte Moderna in 1922, and this probably contributed to his later neglect by publishers and the Brazilian public.

ABOUT THIS BOOK

THE SPHINX ("Esfinge") published in 1908 by Brazil's Coelho Neto, and here translated into English for the first time by Shawn Garrett, is a strange mixture of Symbolist and Occult Novel, concerning a boarding house in Rio de Janeiro whose characters are attracted to, annoyed with or intrigued by their mysterious fellow boarder, Englishman James Marian, who possesses a virile masculine body but the beautiful features of a woman. Our narrator agrees to translate a strange text for Marian, one which reveals his complicated and metaphysical origins, even as tragedy strikes the small compliment of friends and associates. An intriguing, if abstracted, meditation on gender and love, this novel deserves a larger audience. Includes an Afterword by the Translator.

ABOUT THE TRANSLATOR

SHAWN M. GARRETT is the co-editor of PSEUDOPOD.org, the premiere horror fiction podcast, and is either the dumbest smart man or the smartest dumb man you're likely to meet. Thanks to a youth spent in the company of Richard Matheson, Vincent Price, Dr. Shock, Carl Kolchak & Jupiter Jones, he has pursued a life-long interest in the thrilling, the horrific, and the mysterious -- be it in print, film, art or audio. He has worked as a sewerage groundskeeper, audio transcription editor, pornography enabler, and insurance letter writer, and was once paid by Marvel Comics to pastiche the voice of Stan Lee in promotional materials. Shawn spends an inordinate amount of time reading, writing, and watching movies, and has recently translated a number of obscure 19th century French Decadent works for SNUGGLY BOOKS, including **PRINCE NARCISSUS & OTHER STORIES** by Robert Scheffer, **MONADA** by Gabriel Mourey and **WHIMSICAL TALES** by Jean Printemps. He lives near the ocean in a small metal box.

CHAPTER I

The Barkley Inn on Paissandu Street had the honest celebrity of a family home.

Discreet, without any display or even a sign on the granite portal, it was comfortably installed in an old and vast building and seemed to doze in an enchanted sleep under the shade trees at the end of the garden, where a small waterfall built of pebbles cheered the silence with a cool, light, continual murmur of water.

Leafy arbors of jasmine and roses formed pleasant retreats, and the wrens, attracted by the quiet, wove their nests safely in the mossy boughs and hedges of acalipha and cedar. Every morning at breakfast, Miss Barkley (already corseted and with the whole house in order) gave these nests a slow glance, as if considering those fragile baskets of straw and feathers to be rooms also subject to her surveillance. Beyond the building, at the end of an avenue of acacia trees, there was a little cottage that the Englishwoman, with her sober taste and her meticulous cleanliness, had carpeted, furnished and painted for Frederico Brandt, piano teacher, music critic and expert composer.

In that refuge, the artist, who only had the night for studying (because the daylight hours were barely enough for lessons in distant neighborhoods) could, without bothering guests like old Commander Bernaz, practice his classics and, in his moments of genius, compose in the mysterious and nostalgic style of Grieg.

1

Commander Bernaz, with his rheumatism and six hundred-odd stories of interest, was averse to music, and occupied the best rooms at the front of the first floor

Miss Barkley performed with divine silence the marvels of order. At a gesture from her, at the glare of her steely blue eyes that was sharpened even more by her spectacles, the servants bowed without noise, without jostling, each one at her service.

If she surveyed the garden with a slow glance, one would have said that the birds sang more frantically, the roses bloomed more beautifully, and the water from the cascade, always scarce in its timid flow, seemed to run more abundantly and with a louder sound in the damp shadows of the ferns and tinhorão.

She was a thin, angular, stiff woman. Her smooth, amber-colored bandós, drawn back tightly, sharpened her face even more. Her round mouth gave the impression that it was always whistling, her sharp chin turned up as if attracted by her scythe-edged nose.

She hardly spoke and her face, stern and hard, was impervious to a smile.

Décio, a fourth-year student of Medicine, who used to visit the pianist and scandalize the house with his bubbling joy, defined in a simple phrase the upright and withered Englishwoman: "She is a man crippled in a woman." But then, he boasted of having Tennyson's wit, administrative genius, puritanical austerity, and exalted cult.

A craggy soul, apparently barren, a completely bare and dry cliff without edges, Miss Barkley was, however, adored in the neighborhood. At night, figures crept across the garden with packages—it was the poor who came for a daily ration.

#

Finding a room in that simple and modest house was more difficult than the conquest of a well-armed and supplied city.

Miss Barkley would rather keep her rooms empty than rent them out without all the guarantees. She took information and, hearing it, her eyes sparkled as if on fire, clarifying her gossip's saga. Only after convincing herself, with evidence, of the suitor's honesty did she hand him the key, along with the rigid conditions of morality, and a regulatory table with the list of extraordinary ones.

But residence in that house was a high recommendation: the receipt of the "Barkley Pension" was valid as a guarantee in trade, and as a cachet in society.

Despite the manorial vastness of the building, there were few who enjoyed its tranquility, the soft comfort of its maple armchairs, the fragrant whiteness of its linens, its solid and abundant meals, and the flowers from its garden which were never lacking at the dinner table, on the *étagères*, in the guest rooms— and always fresh.

On the first floor, the great hall and two bedrooms were occupied by Commander Bernaz.

Grumpy and homely, always grinding away, he spent his days shut up or, in the great heat, enjoying the mornings and afternoons dressed in white linen and wearing a wide straw hat. He went out into the garden, prowling the shadows, always with a secondhand book or, if near the arbors, to take a nap.

He was the oldest guest. It was even said that he was the one who had advanced the capital to Miss Barkley, for which reason she treated him with intimacy and an almost gentle affection.

Miss Fanny, the teacher, had her room opposite Miss Barkley's—a large room, opening onto the central area, full of potted plants, with a window onto the garden. She spent her days out, taking the afternoons off from her pilgrimage through the neighborhood, spreading the rules of English pronunciation, teaching history, geography, drawing and music to children.

Always with her pocket full of English brochures, when she

saw a small child in some garden she called him and, through the bars, passed him one of the pamphlets, showing him the figures. Sometimes she added colored pencils and cards to the offer and hurried off, stamping her soles stiffly.

On Sundays, she gathered groups of garrulous children, took them to public gardens or the beaches and, laughing happily, with her cheeks blushing and her eyes very bright, she ran with them through the fine grass, between the trees and along the wet sand, strengthening them in the sun, and on the healthy exhalation of the woods or in the salty air that came from the blue ocean.

She had freckles and suffered from migraines, always carrying a small bottle of smelling salts and capsules in her pocket.

At table she spoke English or grudgingly slurred Portuguese, grimacing in disgust, rolling the words in her mouth, as if they were making her sick.

In one of the rooms that opened onto the balcony, Alfredo Penalva, a fifth-year medical student, was very sullen, even though, one morning, the gardener found him snoring in one of the bowers with a package clutched to his chest. As he lifted it into his arms, respectfully calling for decency, the package fell from his hands, came apart, and hard-boiled eggs rolled onto the gravel.

Upstairs, near the staircase, I had my quarters: a sitting room and bedroom. Behind me, in the vast halls, was Péricles de Sá, a widower, building contractor and Sunday photographer. In front, filling the hall and three rooms, including the terrace stocked with tubs and potted plants like a Babylonian garden, was the beautiful and eccentric James Marian.

And there was also Basilio, a bookkeeper... His was an ascetic room on the first floor, which was Miss Barkley's despair because the man insisted on keeping it in disarray, with his scattered books, newspapers, magazines all on the floor. And he yelled when, on entering, he'd found the volumes in order, the newspapers stacked, the magazines in piles, the pipes back on the shelf. Once, he was even about to move because Miss Barkley, in her spirit of order, put an iron bookcase in his room, and patiently, with real pleasure, arranged the books in it.

In the basement, at the front, lived three exemplary young men—one, a law student, Crispim; the two others, brothers, Carlos and Eduardo, from an English family, were employed in an import house.

Miss Barkley got up at five a.m. in the winter and at four in the summer, and by six o'clock the house was glowing.

The guests treated each other with intimacy, and only the Englishman on the second floor, the Apollonian James Marian, withdrew from all conviviality and was always sullen, silent, rarely appearing at the table for mealtime, instead having them alone or in his room when not in the garden, at a small iron table in the shade of the acacia trees, with refreshing *champagne* in a bucket, listening to the birds.

On Sundays, early, dressed all in white, he would go out with a tennis racket or the bag in which he carried his football clothes.

He was, indeed, a handsome young man, tall and strong, erect as a column.

But what immediately surprised, by contrast, in this magnificent athlete was a face of soft and feminine beauty. The limpid forehead, serene and flowered with gold by the rings of hair that rolled gracefully across it, the wide eyes of a thin and sad blue, the straight nose, the small, red mouth, the plump and white neck like a vine, blooming the head of Venus on the massive shoulders of Mars.

The Commander, who didn't see well, just called him "the Puppet," and Basilio, always sour, couldn't stand him, finding him ridiculous with that hairdresser's dummy face.

James had come in with a lord's luggage and great recommendations from Smith & Brothers. Miss Barkley admired him, and at night, on the porch, listened with rapture to him talking about his travels in barbarian lands, in caravans, hunting at great risk in the rushes of India, fighting a black cabilda in Sudan, and all sorts of other adventures and temerities.

He knew the world and all he needed to do was visit one of the poles, to contemplate the cold ends of the earth, hear the bear roar and the reindeer howl on the wandering ice floes.

Guests revolted against James' indifference and dry manners; they thought him uneducated. "If you have pounds, you should eat them," said the commander, "nobody asks for them. The brute! Not even to say 'good morning'... You think you're dealing with the blacks of Africa... You're misguided!"

Miss Fanny intervened, pacifying with her childish voice and her slurred Portuguese: "He is just distinguished. A little shy, ashamed... You should talk with him..."

"Speak? To whom? To the puppet? Really! For God's sake!"

Decio, having lunch one Sunday at the pension, alluded to the handsome Englishman.

"Imagine, the most beautiful head of a woman on the formidable torso of a circus Hercules. Beauty and strength. All Aesthetics!"

"Well, my friend," said the Commander, slowly stirring his potato salad, "that Aesthetic, or whatever you call him, is the biggest boor under the sun."

"Does the Commander know him?"

"Do I know him!? He lives here!"

Décio opened his eyes wide, exclaiming in a shout:

"Here!"

"Yes, sir. Look, ask Miss Barkley."

Miss lowered her eyes, blushing. Still, someone dared to contradict the Commander. It was Frederick Brandt:

"He's not rude, he's just shy." And everyone turned to the pianist, who was helping himself to fish.

"Shy!" exclaimed Basilio, frowning. "Why shy and not rude?"

"I'll explain."

Miss Fanny set down her silverware, interested, and all eyes were fixed on the professor's dark face.

"One night, I was studying Beethoven's *Pathetique*, when I thought I heard walking in the garden, cautious footsteps going away. I ran to the window, opened it, and in the moonlight I recognized Mister James.

"I stood there for a moment, contemplating the night, then I returned to the piano and played until late. When I got up to close the window, he was slowly climbing onto the porch.

"After that night, he never failed to attend my studies and playing. I am certain that he is there in some corner, among the trees, listening to me. He knows me, sees me, and we have met every day. But he has never spoken to me."

"He's a romantic," explained Décio.

"Proud!" cried the bookkeeper.

"What pride? Shyness."

Décio corroborated: "That might be. In general, these colossus are shy and naive like children. True strength is simple as nature. Nature has no obligation to be polite. A man, yes, must be polite. You can see that nobody rebels against the palm trees on the street because they don't move aside to give way or move out of the wet rain, but a man, living among men, has an obligation to be courteous. Now a brute passes by me, very stiff, stamping his feet, without even touching his hat... moving slowly... It's rude! I won't allow it!"

"It's bestial!" summarized Basilio.

A laugh burst out. Pericles de Sá, who had remained silent, cleared his throat. Penalva gasped and began to cough and the two brothers, Carlos and Eduardo, very red, smothered their laughter with their napkins. Miss Barkley frowned resentfully and her flashing eyes shot up to the bookkeeper, who was chewing eagerly.

There was a silence that Brandt interrupted by saying: "I do these things myself. I only speak when I know."

"You? Don't you know us? Doesn't he live here?!" shouted the Commander and Basilio at the same time, with equal fury.

"Yes, but..."

"But what? There's no smoke or fire. You want to make excuses for the man just because he's going to listen to your songs. Why, for God's sake?"

"I don't ask for an audience, Commander. When I want him, I announce a concert."

There was a hiatus of shyness, eyes shifted at the vexed malaise. Miss Barkley recovered:

"Oh, gentlemen, what a discussion! What is this? And such a beautiful day, really... Forget Mister James with his eccentricities. The English are like that, they have fog in their soul. Let the sun come out and you will see them as happy as birds. Let's have lunch in peace."

They were still arguing when the doorbell rang. The servant went up to the second floor and returned to inform Miss Barkley that Mr. James wanted lunch upstairs, and champagne.

The next day, on a misty, windy Monday, Basilio, on his way down to lunch, found Miss Barkley in the hall, where she had her desk protected by a screen, and there was an exchange of words between the two about the scene the day before, at the table.

"You understand. There are young men here, I must maintain respect."

"You're right, Miss, I'm really hot-tempered, it's my genius. But there is no doubt. I will speak no more of the man: he's dead to me. And look, tell Alfredo not to bully me at the table and just leave everything alone."

"It was a defense against disorder."

#

One night I was writing when I thought I heard groans, then the thud of a body, from the Englishman's quarters. I was attentive, listening, but as the moans continued I went out into the hallway and ahead to the door of the hall. It was open, there was light. The moans stopped and I was about to turn back when I saw Mister James appear, paler than ever, his eyes huge, wide with an expression of dread, his mouth half open and his white and beautiful neck bare to the low collar of his silk shirt.

He saw me, ran to me, took both my hands and dragged me to the sofa where he collapsed, gasping. Stunned by such an unforeseen event I was speechless, looking at this man who was struggling, putting his fingers under the collar of his shirt as if to loosen it, shaking his head in anguish, breathing desperately.

Suddenly, staring at me with his great, wonderful eyes, he smiled with feminine sweetness and opened his arms wide on the back of the sofa, his golden head melting down to his chest.

I took his pulse, he was agitated. I touched his forehead, it was cold. I sat down next to him and asked him:

"How do you feel?"

He stirred, stretched out his legs, his teeth clicked.

On the table was a bottle and glasses: whiskey. I prepared it with water and offered it to him. He drank in evenly spaced sips. He was inert for some time, eyes closed as if asleep, breathing with difficulty, but little by little regaining his calm, smiling in ecstasy, murmuring vague words, he began to pass his hand over his chest. He jumped up and, very gently, very affectionately, shook my hand. "Thank you... Thank you...!" He remained silent for some time, keeping my hand in his, and at last he turned away, began to walk through the hall and reached the threshold of the terrace where he retreated hesitantly, looking about wildly and smiling.

I said goodbye, offering myself for whatever help he might need. He accompanied me to the door, very grateful, explaining that he was "subject to attacks of vertigo." And as he shook my hand effusively, he was smiling and saying in English "Thanks! Thanks!"

I retired to my quarters, and that night I could not carry on with the work at hand. I sat at the window smoking, I read, I lay down sleepless, worried about the man, and then it was dawn—the street was starting to move—when I fell asleep.

In the morning, crossing the alley of acacia trees on the way to the bathroom, I discovered James in the middle of the garden, following with interest the comings and goings of a wren that was settling on a branch, weaving its nest.

Hearing my footsteps he turned his face away. I was about to speak to him when I saw him slowly walking away, his arms behind his back, his head down.

Such indifference outraged me. The Commander and Basilio were decidedly right.

And we didn't meet again. From my room, at night, I could hear his footsteps until late, sometimes humming to himself; nothing more.

#

One night, Brandt and I were walking on the beach of Botafogo when we saw him drive by in an open car.

"There goes the eccentric," said the musician, tossing the end of his cigar into the street. We talked about his mysterious life and I mentioned the event of the other night and The Puppet's "vertigo." Brandt, after listening to me in silence, said:

"To me, he seems a sick person. I want you to see him at night, when I play. The man comes to my window and stays there for hours and hours, listening. There are certain songs that irritate him, I don't know why. As soon as I start them, he leaves, nervous, muttering. Others attract him, like Meyer-Helmund's *Melodie Nocturne*, for example, and it wouldn't surprise me to see him, one night, enter the chalet, listen, and then leave without a word. Beethoven and Schumann exercise real prestige over him. If you want to convince yourself come to the chalet and you will see. And the most interesting thing is that Miss Fanny adores him."

"Who? Miss Fanny!"

"Yes. I don't even know if the man stays in the garden to listen to me or if my piano is just a pretext. They talk, walk together. I see them walking around until late."

"Miss Fanny!"

"Should I continue?"

"Oh!... It's not possible. Miss Fanny? I don't believe it."

"If you would like to convince yourself..."

"Tomorrow then...!"

"Come tomorrow. Early. At nine."

"So I shall."

And we said goodbye. Brandt was attending a rich birthday party, on the program to play an *Elegia* and the *Marcha dos Mistas*.

The night was stifling. In the distance, over the oily sea, lightning flashed illuminating the dense and turbulent sky. Gusts of wind raised whirlwinds of dust.

#

The following night, at the agreed time, I entered the chalet. Brandt was waiting for me, vaguely leafing through the score for *Parsifal*.

The arrangement of the room revealed the artist. Ample, soft and comfortable furniture: ottomans and divans in green Morocco, with piled pillows, an open Bechstein grand piano and a harmonium. A tall screen made of jacaranda and silk, inlaid with gold embroidery, depicted a ghostly riverside landscape full of distant storks, some standing on one leg, gazing thoughtfully at the trembling threads of water. A fluffy purple carpet drowned the footsteps, silencing all noise.

In a pot, on a faience column, a slender palm tree gracefully tilted its fan-like leaves and on the walls were precious paintings, engravings, portraits, frowning samurai masks, and ancient porcelain. An authentic panoply arranged around a shield with a visorless helmet at the top and, radiating like trophies, indigenous arrows, blowpipes, clubs and borés, all arranged around an eye-catching feather headdress flanked by a tucum belt fringed with coconut bells and a shiny head of hair, black, long, flowing like the full tail of a wild foal.

The music shelves were choked with albums. A green curtain covered the bedroom door.

Brandt opened one of the shutters and then a branch of jasmine, starred with flowers, leaned intimately into the room.

The moonlight looked like snow.

Outside, in the yard, the trees made a whisper of rumpled silks, and at intervals, high-pitched yells pierced the silence. Somewhere in the neighborhood, a lady sang in hysterical falsetto.

Brandt smiled and, taking an album from the shelf, opened it at the piano and sat down, saying to me serenely:

"I will lure him."

He ran his fingers along the keyboard, withdrawn for a moment, his eyes held high as if waiting for inspiration...

His fingers moved lightly, serenely, drawing from his soul that gentle *Pastoral* by Beethoven. The sounds were singing, spreading the divine poetry, opening the feeling to the mystery of nature, flying like dream butterflies into the dozing night, mingling with the perfume outside in the mystical serenity of sleeping space in the moonlight.

The reason for that enchantment, the reason for that harmonious celebration, disappeared from my memory when the pianist who, occasionally bending down and casting his eyes to the garden, warned me, injected more soul into the wonderful symphony: "Here he comes!"

I occupied the armchair opposite the window and I distinctly saw the white figure advance, now in full light, now veiled by the shadow of the languid branches.

I sat up in my armchair to see better. Nothing. I went forward to the window and looked: there he was motionless, beside a palm tree, listening.

In the distance, another white figure, light as the morning mist, seemed to sway at the end of the acacia alley as if turning in a slow twirl. It was Miss Fanny. And so they were both there while the music sounded.

When the piano silenced, James left his post and walked slowly towards the teacher. They seemed like pale visions, lost in the shadows, flanking the arbors that the moonlight smothered.

"You're right. It's an idyll."

"Are you convinced?"

"It is true."

"You can see that the Englishman isn't as eccentric as he seems."

"More than it looks, Brandt. Beautiful as he is, with his fortune, he could lift his heart higher and give his eyes to a charming, divine face. Miss Fanny... you'll agree... Excellent girl, no doubt about it, but..."

"Who knows why! Miss Fanny is intelligent, she has hair that transfigures her and love is content with little. There are those who concentrate passion in a smile, in a gesture, in the sound of the voice, abstracting everything else. Pain is sometimes loved. Who knows why! Pure souls run deeper. Neither is vulgar: he is eccentric; she idealistic. Beauty is vain. The heart does not see, it feels. Sight is of intelligence, not of feeling. It is in the head... and the head is what exists in reality. The heart, which plunges into the mystery, is the rhythm. Who knows where! But let's get away from it. Now Schumann, the *Reverie.*"

"And *prelude.*"

Again, in the moonlight, the two figures approached. Slowly and thoughtfully, James, detaching himself from his companion, came to stand by the palm tree, and Miss Fanny stood where she had appeared, motionless and white, as of marble.

At the end of the heartfelt piece, James silently resumed his path to join the teacher and, blending into a single blur, they disappeared into the shadows.

"It's curious!"

"Why do you say that?

"I don't know."

The night was late, serene and caressing, with the moonlight becoming more and more white like a flower opening in silence. The fresh breeze stirred the branches, shaking the fertile or virgin flowers that they loved, spreading aroma or receiving pollen. The perfume rose in a voluptuous serenade: it was the nuptial hymn of sensual roses, the epithalamus of magnolias and jasmine, the divine harmony of corollas.

The branches stooped languidly, and the black shadows of the branches, moving on the sand of the paths, were like watchmen of love, discreetly hiding the night's colloquy.

Brandt, at the window, repeated the phrase:

"Who knows where! It can be pure spiritual love, that divine affinity that establishes currents of attraction between distant souls, making a blond man leave the frigid North for the brown arms of a daughter from the land of the sun. The people call this mysterious force—Fate. And why not—Sympathy? Beauty is an illusion of the senses. Beautiful, truly Beautiful is the Ideal only. The bride of Menippus is a symbol. There is no beauty that resists Time, and Beauty is eternal like Being.

"I tell you: there are times when I feel passionately in love and the Woman I love (let's call her Woman, which is the expression of the feminine) does not live, just exists. She is immaterial and I feel her. I see it in a wave of sounds like the smoke rising from thuribles. It envelops me with her essence and gives me pure spiritual joy, which is ecstasy, sweeter, more fruitful than the ephemeral spasm that generates death. It's the Melody, you'll say. I don't know, I call it Love. Have you never loved?"

"Truly, never. I have had fleeting impressions."

"Fleeting... Love is a fixed idea: it rises from the heart in feeling and becomes thought in the brain. Who knows where? This man perhaps found in Miss Fanny the complement of his being, his feminine. They were two desires that sought each other in the Ideal. Don't palm trees love from a distance?"

"And have you noticed, Frederick, that James' face has not a single manly feature?"

"A Sphinx face, my friend."

"Well put: the face of a sphinx. Good night, Brandt. And thanks for the show."

"If you liked it, come back."

And at the door he added: "I still hope to drag you here. Orpheus tamed wild beasts, stopped the course of rivers with his mystical lyre. It's not much for me to overwhelm a soul."

"You have an all-powerful Art. See you tomorrow."

I reached the bright, glowing porch when the silence broke into sounds of tender and touching sweetness. I leaned against the balustrade, listening. It was Elsa's "*Arioso*", the description of the dream, the humble song of Fragility strengthened by Faith, on the banks of the Scalda, between the perfidious cruelty of Frederico and Ortruda and the indifference of the *brabanções*. Where did it come from? What voice spread it through the night with such sweet tenderness?

But suddenly, a strange exclamation chilled me:

"O my soul! Where art thou, my soul...!"

I glanced in the song's direction and saw the white figure of James by the bower, his arms raised to the sky in supplication, and, lying on the edge of a flower bed, like a ruin, Miss Fanny was crying.

CHAPTER II

One morning, in an auspicious uproar, Alfredo came into my room with a smile and, still at the door, panting, announced that the Englishman was going to have lunch downstairs with us.

It was he who had carried the message. Miss Barkley had been moved: she had spread out flowers on the table, brought tubs of plants up from the garden, and was hanging around the cook, arranging dishes, recommending the seasoning of the meats and the freshness of the eggs and lettuce so that they would taste good to the difficult man. Two bottles of champagne were chilling in the fridge and the sweat that was soaking through Miss Barkley's clothes, and smearing her hair, was from the race she made to Largo do Machado to look for mutton chops, and fruit for dessert.

"But... at the common table?" I asked with interest and incredulity, and Alfredo, with his broom and a cloth under his arm, said:

"Yes sir. And he's already down there, on the balcony with a book, for quite a while.

What a pity it wasn't Sunday for everyone to enjoy the surprise. How Basilio, Pericles, Brandt, Penalva, Crispim and the two inseparable brothers would feel when they heard about the big event. And Miss Fanny, poor thing! She was out chatting with the children, from house to house, drawing landscapes, babbling sonatas with him in her thoughts, anxiously awaiting the night.

Only old Bernaz and I would have the incomparable fortune to see the divine young man nibble on the pressed ham, drink the wine, chew the grapes, sip the coffee, and maybe we enjoy the sound of his voice.

I went down at the first ring of the bell, which the butler was ringing in a fury of alarm, and I soon noticed the great changes in the room: happier with the freshness of the palm trees, with the vivid color of the still dewy roses, with the cerulean shine of the crystals and, in the center of the table, resplendent, laden with flowers, a silver boat among festive trappings.

Miss Barkley, very slender and stiff, with her glossy bandós on boards, came and went, sluggish and silent, her spectacles gleaming intently and her nimble fingers incessantly arranging, arranging, straightening up—here, a napkin; there, some silverware; over here, a flower.

On the embroidered tablecloth were spread cloth napkins, interspersed with silk and gold, in the opulence of a feast. Bottles were lined up on the buffet, and the crystal ice bucket showed its claws.

James, on the porch in a striped flannel costume, relaxed in a wicker chair, reading a brochure.

I passed him indifferently and headed for the stairs, admiring the purity of the blue sky and the brightness of the palm trees in the sun, when I sensed him get up and follow me; at last he called to me politely. When I turned around, I found him with his hand outstretched, and his handsome face, skin as white and fine as jasper under which a youthful blood flowed in roses, was charming and covered with a smile.

Our handshake was truly affectionate. We stared at each other, not saying a word: he was blushing, I felt myself turning pale, and as surprise stopped me at the top of the stairs, he bowed gently and, with a graceful gesture, invited me down, yielding to me the first step.

Together, like close friends, we went out into the garden where the little waterfall (another kindness from Miss Barkley) gushed in abundance.

The gardener, who was shearing the grass in the flowerbeds, balancing his body in rhythm as he swung the cutlass, stopped suddenly, astonished, and, humbly taking off his hat, stood looking at us, his cigarette dangling from the corner of his mouth.

The commander's bald head, shining through the half-opened leaves of a window, did not go unnoticed, following us with astonished curiosity, as we walked slowly, talking, among the cut rosebushes.

Cicadas sang loudly, butterflies fluttered or perched on trembling stems, and the sun, glistening on the sand, languidly softened the foliage under the weight of voluptuous fatigue.

And James, in his soft, caressing voice, asked me if I could translate from English a piece of writing, a kind of novel...

"An extravagance."

"I may assist you."

He took my arm and I, increasingly bewildered, trembling as if I were being dragged by an assassin into a back alley, far from all help, was intimately enchanted by the proposal that left me on the threshold of the arcane, binding me, by intelligence, to that strange man, whose beauty was a mystery, greater, perhaps, than his eccentricities.

"I have the manuscript. The handwriting is uneven, not always clear, but as our rooms are adjacent—no doubt, isn't it true? I don't care about the price."

"Price?"

"The price. Of course, the work is difficult, very difficult."

"No, sir, I don't usually translate. I have never translated and if I make an exception it is out of sympathy for the work, with no other interest."

"Oh! No, no...! The work is difficult, very difficult."

"So much the better, I will gain from it by improving my English."

"Oh...! It's my own English..."

"Is it a novel then?"

He stopped, transfigured, his mouth half-open, looking at me with his big sad eyes, and after a moment he said in a vague, subtle tone, as if in love's confidence:

"It's... my... novella."

A shiver ran down my spine. In a deaf and trembling voice I asked:

"It must be pretty!"

He blushed, shrugged his shoulders, pursed his lips, and, as if for air, shook his head, which shone like gold, anxiously in the sun.

"Well, I'm at your command."

"When do you want to start?"

"Whenever you'd like."

"Tomorrow...?"

"Yes, tomorrow."

"Is very difficult!" he repeated, crestfallen. "Very difficult!"

The third ringing of the bell took us back. Miss Barkley, leaning out on the porch, was looking out over the garden, and when she saw us appear, she gave vent to her surprise:

"Oh! I didn't know you knew each other."

"Yes, Miss... well, one night..."

Old Bernaz, who had put on his frock coat, frowned, grimacing at his stinging calluses, and I didn't miss the look of hatred he gave me, as if I were a traitor, seeing me with the Englishman. James bowed before him, getting only a grumpy grunt in response. And we sat down at the fragrant table.

James, struggling with the Portuguese, praised the flowers with exultation, and kindly offered roses to Miss Barkley, who stuck them in her bodice. I myself got one in my buttonhole. The Commander left his own, an admirable Vermerol, laying on the towel. James took a Paul Neyron for himself.

Lunch went well. Miss Barkley was expansive. The servant poured the champagne, but when he brought the bottle to the Commander, the uncompromising man spread his bulging hand over the glass, refusing.

"Do you not drink?" James asked.

And the old man, without lifting his head, snorted:

"Water."

Then he mentioned the rest room. But over coffee, he broke down in rasping, broken French, talking about the radiant beauty of the day, the cicadas, the heat and, on the subject of the tasteless grapes, he recalled his abundant Douro river.

"Yes, many grapes over there! James should know that, because the wines of the best Portuguese vintage are aged in London's vast cellars."

"Oh! Yes... the port..."

"Port and the others, the good ones. In Portugal, only the dregs remain."

We left the table at two o'clock, softened, and as James passed onto the porch with Miss Barkley, the Commander, advancing on tiptoe, crossed his arms before me, and, patting his belly, asked with a great wet pout and his eyes very naughty:

"But what have you to say to me? Explain this thing to me..."

"The man became personable, Commander."

"He got his ducks in a row, didn't I tell you?" And clutching my arm, secretly: "And look, he's really nice. Today, I noticed. A woman's face, you are right. A beautiful woman's face! And Miss Fanny caught him, eh? She's got him by the leg."

And he snorted a mocking laugh.

#

Dinner that day, in spite of the redoubled activity of Miss Barkley, who did not rest for a second helping the servants, was not served until seven o'clock, in the unusual glow of all the gas burners.

The table, more extended and richer, gave a solemn appearance to the room, between the luminous glow of the buffet and carving mirrors. Sometimes, in the breath of the breeze that stirred the palms of the arecas and latanias, there were light murmurs of brambles.

Guests, informed of the big event at lunch, hummed and whispered as they strolled along the porch. Decius, who had appeared noisily and with a great yearning for art, appealed to the "stupendous" Frederick, evoker of Thracian melodies, gushed out compliments for James, the Breton Apollo who, tired of languid Olympus and insipid ambrosia, had descended to fraternize with mortals, eating at the table, with human appetite, the cow stew and the leaves of the vegetable gardens.

Pericles, desolate, regretted finding himself unprepared for plates, otherwise he would have perpetuated James' appearance in an instant.

"What if we sang *God Save The King*!?" Decius cried.

But Penalva got ahead of him:

"No making fun of this man. It's terrible!"

"Who?" asked Basilio, in a contemptuous tone.

"Who? James Marian. Do you know of Félix Alvear? He's a

colossus."

Everyone agreed.

"A monster!" added Decio, his eyes widening.

"Well, on Sunday after the game at *Fluminense*, Félix was about to kiss Marian, calling him *Miss*, he put his hands on his chest and, as Alvear charged, he threw a punch, bloodying his face. The funny thing is that, later, Marian fainted."

"Sissy!" scoffed Basilio. "It's just that there wasn't one there who knew the truth. Nothing will change. The recipient is knocked down or he's head over heels. It's over in a moment. Let him mess with me."

"You...?" and Décio spread his hands in capoeira gestures.

"I know, I know a little; I defend myself. I am a man! Today, I am tired... Even so, not just anyone steps up."

When Crispim appeared, very shy, chuckling, buttoning his alpaca jacket, Basilio muttered: "Here comes the spinach!" Everyone chuckled, dispersing, and the student, very thin, freckled, with his *pince-nez* mounted on his peaked nose and his hair ruffled, passed in silence while rubbing his hands and hesitating among the guests. Crispim approached Carlos and talked to him softly, in a whisper, about the beauty of the sunset and the perfume that rose from the garden where the water from the fountain ruffled over the foliage.

The Commander, in a frock coat, arrived at the door and bowed, waving to everyone with an open hand.

"Good afternoon, Commander."

"Hot, huh?"

"Horrible!"

But Miss Fanny, coming up from the garden in white, with

23

an orchid in her bodice, stopped the murmuring. They made room and she passed lightly, grateful and flushed. The third ring sounded and Miss Barkley appeared very stiff and, with a sweet look, invited them all:

"Let's go?"

But they hesitated.

"And Mr. James?" asked the Commander.

Miss Barkley smiled, shrugged:

"He's upset. He had a disappointment."

Basilio muttered: "He's drunk."

They entered in silence, sat down, and the servant began to serve the soup, when Miss Fanny, nodding this way and that, got up, covering her mouth with her handkerchief. The bookkeeper was looking at her sideways and, when she disappeared down the hall, he growled to Décio:

"Consumption, my friend. It comes. This year she will sing Christmas songs from underground in a horrible voice! Also... there's less of a grimace."

At the fish, the teacher reappeared, paler, and without the orchid. She sat up sheepishly. Every now and then she gasped a longing breath from her lap, bringing the handkerchief to her mouth.

The dinner grew cold. Apart from the clink of silverware, nothing else broke the heavy silence. No one dared to tackle a subject; conversation was whispered, in shy secrecy, between two. Sometimes a smile roamed the table. Basilio himself, always snarling with sarcasm, devoured it silently, with a splash of voracious jaws.

Suddenly and violently starting, pushing back his chair,

Décio stood up, his arms extended out, in an attitude of adoration and rapture. Everyone, in mute amazement, followed his dazzled gaze.

The moon's light was falling sweetly, covering the trees with a silver mist, whitewashing the veranda, entering the living room. One of the palm trees, at the door, gleamed, and Décio, with fixed eyes, greeted with rapture:

"'Oh Rabbetna... Baalet!... Tanit!... Anaitis!... Astarte! Derceto! Ashtoreth! Mylitta! Athara! Elissa! Tiratha! By the hidden symbols, by the resounding sistrums, by the furrows of the earth, by the eternal silence, and by the eternal fecundity, dominator of the dark sea and the bluish shores, O Queen of damp things, save us.'" And for a moment still he maintained the contemplative attitude. At last, sitting down and helping himself to roast, he exclaimed:

"Amazing!"

And laughed. Miss Barkley nodded condescendingly.

"Is that yours?" asked Penalva.

"Mine?!" and Décio's lively eyes, fixed on his colleague, flashed. "Barbarian! You don't know genius? That is from the divine Flaubert. It is the invocation from *Salammbô*." And, facing the still white night of soft heat, touched by the scent of the magnolias, he raised the glass to the full length of his arm, and exclaimed: "On ice!"

"A great memory!" complimented the Commander.

"Extraordinary!" Penalva confirmed. "He recites pages and pages. Verses, even... knows entire volumes by heart. Baudelaire, for example... just ask for a recitation."

"Not so much as that, my dear,"—the student countered, with modesty. "I know some poetry." But then, he was excited: "Anyone who doesn't glorify Baudelaire doesn't feel, or he doesn't have a soul."

"Excuse me, my friend," interrupted the Commander, spreading his hands "I am a creature like you, I mean: I have a soul, the proof is that I am a Christian and here I tell you: in things of memory I am like a stone."

Basilio smiled fiercely and, rolling bread balls, asked, without lifting his head:

"And numbers, Commander? How are you with figures?"

"Sure, by will and by practice. But in high school... History, for example. I could never deal with that. Mixed up the kings, made a hell of a mess. I got lost in the Crusades."

"But he found himself in the crusaders," Basilio ventured, rubbing his fingers.

The laughter exploded irresistibly and the Commander, with a little yellow laugh, rolled up his napkin, responded with an answer that was lost. Miss Fanny went to Decio, gently pushing aside the roses in a vase that hid him.

"And Tennyson? Do you know anything of his, doctor?"

"Oh! Miss... unfortunately..." and shook his head in denial. "I only know a small amount of English."

"Oh! Tennyson..." exclaimed the teacher, her eyes darting.

"Tennyson!" repeated Miss Barkley, ecstatic, and rising, proposed coffee on the porch in the moonlight. It was a divine night.

"Admirable."

And they left. The lecture, although interesting and pleasant, under the charm of the night that had refreshed me, did not attract me. They laughed and I, with my thoughts far away, sometimes thought I had been struck by some allusion and distrust, spurring revolt. Pericles noticed my detachment and, slapping my thigh, said:

"You're worried, man."

"Distracted..."

In vain, Décio recited with his cadent voice, faithful to the rhythm, fine-tuning the rhymes, highlighting the images. In vain, his spirit overflowed in shams mocking literacy, exposing the ridiculousness of disgraceful elegance, commenting on the futile mimicry of the native, the pegs of fashion forced by insisting on the *precious* work from the simple habits of our lives. They laughed, though I remained indifferent. It was just that I was thinking of the manuscript that had been promised to me and that I had hoped to find on my desk, to take a path through it, searching in the web of punctuation for a trace that would lead me to the mystery of that indecipherable soul and, perhaps, who knows? To ideas of a female head clumsily implanted on a masculine body, making one think of a robust Monkeypot tree whose branches were a rosebush.

When Brandt, rising with a sigh of relief, invited me to the chalet, I declined on the grounds of "illness."

"Music is a balm. Remember Saul," Penalva said.

And Decio added, seductively: "And today we're going to have the Summoning of *Eurydice*. Do you still resist?

"I am sick."

"Are you going to bed?"

"Perhaps."

"It's monstrous! On a night like this it becomes infamy!"

"I'm feeling badly."

"Well, go ahead! And may nightmares haunt you."

And the group descended, boisterous and joyful, and went through the garden, to the sound of Decio's voice declaiming, among the golden acacias:

Ce ne seront jamais ces beautés de vignettes.
Produits avariés, nés d'un siècle vaurien...

(*It will never be these thumbnail beauties.*
Spoiled products, born of a rascal century)

Basilio stretched out his legs, huffing:

"Now we can enjoy the night."

Crispim and the brothers Carlos and Eduardo went down: the first, to his books; the other two for the walk they took every night along the Avenida to Botafogo. The refreshed Commander, hands clasped on his belly, rolled his fingers. The two Misses whispered at the balustrade. A gas burner just lit the room.

Pericles approached politics and soon the lamentations and the ominous omens began and, in the serenity of the moonlight while the flowers exhaled, the Fatherland, disintegrated from its foundations, tumbled away crumbling in rumors, chewed up by sharp edges, debased, insolvable, disappearing ruined into a bottomless abyss—which was the maw of the Englishman. I left, bored.

When I entered my sitting room, all covered in moonlight, my heart thudded with a foreboding crash. I turned, glancing across the deserted interior. The sounds of Brandt's piano came to me softened by distance. I struck a match, lit the gas which killed the astral light, and stood before the table, absorbed, forgetting everything.

Why shouldn't I converse with James? My hesitancy knew no reason after the morning we had spent together in almost confidential intimacy. I dared and, stepping resolutely out into the hall, walked straight to his hall door.

It was half-open and the vast room, silent, with no other light than the moonlight, seemed funerary to me.

The impulse of spirits that had brought me there slackened into cowardice. Even so, I struggled against the cowardly shyness that drew me to my bare rooms, so sad without those promised pages that I longed for, and towards which all the energies of my soul moved in mysterious attraction.

I gently pushed open the door. A dry crack sounded. I drew back with a shudder, under the impression of a shiver; but I insisted. The door gave way, opening onto the pale hall in the moonlight from the terrace. The air reached me in gusts and flowed down the hall. I clapped my hands, timidly at first, weakly, then louder, and it seemed to me that the house was roaring with resounding echoes.

A white figure appeared as an apparition. He advanced with slow theatrical steps and, at the center table, stopped with his head down, clasping his hands together. Suddenly, throwing his arms up violently, throwing his head back, he shook it in a desperate gesture, repeating, in a hollow voice, the exclamation that, one night, I had heard in the garden:

"O my soul! Where art thou, my soul!"

I recognized James. I pushed harder. He whirled around, lunging for the door. So I strode forward and the young man, as if caught in an unworthy act, withdrew, retreated into a corner, where he fell, terrified and mute, his arms rigidly outstretched in repulsion.

I called him once, twice: "Mister James! Mister James!" Then, recognizing my voice, he approached beaming, his friendly hands open, welcoming me with affectionate effusion. In the light his enigmatic face glowed like marble.

He put his arm around my shoulders. A fine aroma wafted from his body, and his breath, which washed over my face, was warm and aromatic. Caressing me with a lover's blandishments, he led me to the terrace and there, among the plants, in the open air, we sat down.

Again he took my hands—his were freezing cold—and looked at me closely, with the terrifying eyes of someone trying to extort a secret. But sweetly, a smile broke out on his face... A smile... why should I alter my impression?... enamored. And then I had the certainty, the painful, poignant certainty that the soul of that man, which shone in beauty, was... what to say?

I asked him about the novel. He jumped up, startled, and quickly passed into the parlor, turned on the gas, turned on all the lights on the chandelier, and disappeared into the bedroom, the entrance to which was concealed by a heavy pearl-colored silk curtain, the same as those on the doors that opened onto the terrace.

It lingered long enough for me to examine the richly and tastefully, if extravagantly, furnished room.

A group of Louis XV, in yellow brocade, made up one of the corners, under the modesty of a clear screen flowered with lilacs. At the opposite angle was an oriental softness: on a Carmanian rug, limp cushions, concave stools, ottomans invited voluptuous stretches. Two wide ebony chairs carved in flowers and lace, with a back made by the open tail of a peacock whose plumage was exquisitely inlaid, offered in bloody damask the delight of open quilts which, yielding to the slightest pressure, warmed the children's velvet cushioned feet.

And, in a gap, with satin pillows covered by a gold-colored strangle, magazines were scattered and still rolled in disarray on the white bearskin that was stretched out at his feet. Two pans on tripods gave off a vague aroma of incense.

And naked, airy, on an onyx column, a flexible marble *bayadera*, her eyes half-closed, smiling, her bust curved, her firm breasts in the air, she arched her arms above her head playing a sistrum, her tiny foot badly planted on the ground, rehearsing the light step of a languid ballet.

Two plinths stood tall and gilded, with *tremós* in wide

frames in which curled little angel heads smiled between the leaves and in the center, under the bronze chandelier, the antique table, with twisted columns around which vast and fat burgundy Morocco armchairs opened up to the sensual softness of laps.

There were flowers in profusion. They were forgotten in vases by the chairs, dying on the plinths, and one's feet pressed against loose petals, wilted bouquets, dried roses, all elastic as cloth.

On the table a wide and thick leather-covered volume attracted my keen curiosity. I opened it.

The leaves, old, grimy parchment, crackled, creaked like tin sheets. On the frontispiece, two lilies clung to the same stem—one erect, in a starry bell, the other martyred, hanging in languor, and surmounted by a dripping heart pierced by an arrow.

I turned the page and the text appeared in bizarre arabesques, with irregular shapes and complicated combinations: discs and sigmoids, wedge-shaped rods crossing or flanking Greek hemicycles in a descending shape, curved over the quivering line that, among the Egyptians, was the symbol of water, dots, chips, quotation marks and scrolls. Sometimes truncated profiles of men, animals, objects—a complex ideogram, a vast enigma of arcane or morbid fantasy.

I was still leafing through the weird volume when James appeared hugging a leather briefcase. Surprising me, in my curious examination, he rushed forward and, trembling, with a voice that quavered, spread his hand over the open page:

"You see? You know...?"

"No. What is it?" I asked, counting on an explanation.

James was silent, eyes fixed on the book. At last he said with a dismayed expression:

"Nobody knows! So, in vain, I have tried all the climates of this vast earth. For six years, in the hope of resolving these griffins,

I went through the places where, in deep spirits, the science of the gods still exists. I have visited the dark temples that the earth is beginning to devour, I have entered the woods where they lie, as if rooted, with wild grass growing around them. Vipers in the thick weeds, parasites blooming their parched shoulders, the yogis and the sadhus were paralyzed in ecstasy. I climbed, by rough paths, the steep cold mountains where the mahatmas walk unconscious centuries, in an existence in which the hours do not enter. I spoke, in caves, to hermits older than the forests... and they all dismissed me without hope. In Europe, this volume was examined by Rawlinson, Ebers, Oppert, Maspero, Erman and many, many others! Some smiled, taking me for crazy, others rejected me, offended, judging me to be a mystifier. I spent thousands of pounds... In vain! And I would give as much as I have, I would give a drop of blood per word to whoever could tear me away from these symbols that torture me."

"And where did you find this book?"

"Where? By my side, in life."

"Who composed it?"

"Arhat."

Saying that name, he shuddered as if in shock and threw the text on the table, starting to walk restlessly, shuddering. He exhaled: "Nobody knows!" But then, calming down, he smiled, and sadness clouded his smile, saying in calm words: "And who knows the story of your soul? Who?! Everyone has a book like this—visible or invisible, right? That's life: we have it under our eyes and we don't decipher it... and it devours us. It's the Sphinx. Turn this book forward a page—it is tomorrow, the mystery of life. Flip it backwards, still mystery! The past, death. The present, what is it? Redoubled, in which we swing between longing and hope. And so, what is it worth knowing? Close the volume or leave it open. In sleep or waking life is always indecipherable.

"But close it. So that it's like an abyss whose bottom you

can't see. It makes you dizzy. Close it! The night is beautiful!" And he walked to the terrace.

I asked him about the novel.

"It's over there in that folder. You can take it. The ending is missing."

"Didn't you finish it?"

He paled, and suddenly, as he was within reach of the chandelier, he shut off all the lights. And the moonlight, again, spread its spiritual clarity.

Then, catching me by the arm, he snuggled up to me, casting a pallid look around. I could feel his panting and the rapid beating of his heart.

The tall palm trees on the street gleamed, waving their leaves in soft, whispering motion; people passed, sometimes cars. Piano sounds came from afar, now vague, now vibrating clearly. James listened. Suddenly, walking away in his thoughtful stride, with long paces, he repeated:

"The ending... You'll have it soon enough. I've been hesitating a lot, but it needs to end. Maybe this day. The night is beautiful." He stared up at the sky. "Maybe today!" He leaned over the railing, showing me the white shape in the bower. I recognized the teacher.

"Miss Fanny?"

He nodded, with an enigmatic smile, and murmured:

"Captive..."

"By who?"

He limited himself to pointing to the Englishwoman. He was silent for a moment, then, in slow words, as if he had mentally set them in a melancholy rhythm, he daydreamed:

"Imagine a lioness taken to the desert in a cage from which the iron rods would break with just the brush of her body. Would she flee to her lair, lured by the resinous scent of the jungle and the roar of heroic lions?"

"Undoubtedly."

"No."

"Why?"

"I would do the opposite: I would reinforce the cage with my own body, I would close my eyes so as not to see the desert, I would make myself deaf to the seductive voices, I would let myself die holding my breath so as not to inhale the musk and the acrid smell of the forests. I would do so... if I were virtuous."

Miss Fanny was coming out of the bower. She stopped for a moment, thinking, picked a flower and walked slowly towards the acacia alley. James muttered:

"Poor lioness!"

Noticing, however, my astonishment, he explained, without turning around, always leaning over the parapet and with the same leisure:

"Arhat used symbols as an expression of the mystery. What cannot be said or represented, is figured. Color is a symbol for the eyes, sound is a symbol for the ears, aroma is a symbol for the sense of smell, endurance is a symbol for touch. Life itself is a symbol. The truth, who knows it? The key of symbols would open the golden door of Science, of the true and only Science, which is the knowledge of the cause."

He didn't speak to me, but to the night, tossing the words as if they were petals that he slowly spread into the air.

Even though the conviction that I was speaking to a madman was more and more affirmed in my mind, I was interested in that extravagant discourse that took me out of the orderly world and threw me into the frenzied fantasy of the degenerated—a warm, somber forest, vented itself here and there in luminous clearings where the predestined falter and leap the trees of the dream from which they make the lyres of Poetry, the idols and the altars of Religions.

"Are you from London?"

"From London?" He shrugged. "I don't know. I grew up near London. I was never told where I was born."

"And your parents?"

"I don't know. I never saw them. Mother... What a sweet word! I got used to bringing it to my lips as something that eluded my thirst for love. I lived on the scent of an unknown flower, do you understand?" He sat down and, head lowered, his hands hanging between his knees, his chest bent, he continued: "You come straight to my heart with a talisman of Kindness. And you are able to penetrate it."

"And you don't trust me? You can believe in me."

He cut me off with a gesture:

"If I didn't trust you, I wouldn't have received you. And do you know why I trust? Because trust is the purest form, the concentrate of dreams. There are two kinds of men who live alone— the egoist and the thinker: the former withdraws like the octopus— calling all good to himself; the second is isolated to contemplate. One locks himself in the shadows, the other seeks reflection: it is like someone who sits on the edge of a lake, seeing in the waters the images of heaven and earth, along with his own. The isolated are, in general, naive and good: as they do not dispense trust, they do not reap disappointment. So what can you do? The world lives with you, and that's a lot. Whoever gives himself completely to the world forgets his own being.

"I knew men, and in them I found the tiger, the dog, the fox, and the viper: the sadist, the flatterer, the trickster, and the ungrateful. You are one of those who hear in silence and see in darkness. Do you think I haven't seen you late at night at the window? For what? For dreams. The dream is fecundity, it is like the pollen of flowers—it flies, but it is not lost. It is not possible that pollen has more vital energy than thought and the pollen flies in space, cross each other in the open air and fertilize. Besides, you speak English, and understand me. Other than the ladies, you're the only one I can communicate with. Remember our first encounter?"

"Yes, I remember."

"I was coming out of a crisis, recovering from an 'aura', and you accompanied me, encouraged me. I owe you this kindness. The most..."

"You're incorrect, Mister James. If others don't engage you, it's because they see you as withdrawn. Everyone here loves you..."

"Me?! Do you love me...? Why? What have I done for them? They're curious about me, that's what you mean. They want to penetrate me, see what I have in my soul. I have always avoided friendship so as not to suffer. If I found it real, I might lose it and be a wretch; if they betrayed me... I don't know. I had a protector, Arhat. I lived with him and he watched over me. It was not love that surrounded me, but care. I was his workmanship, the work of his knowledge. He had great zeal for me, always attentive to my health, to my sorrows, medicating me, defending me from all evil so that I could resist. I was to him like a delicate object kept in a display case. There was no love. What has he done for me? He gave me life, educated me and made me heir to the fortune I squander. I was sleeping and he woke me up... and now I'm sleepy, just wanting to get back to sleep. Give me your hand."

I gave it and he took it to his neck, turning it with him, just below his shoulders, making me feel the soft, cold flesh that my fingers treasured. He paused my fingers in a furrow and, following it, I felt the presence of a large suture, like an eruption of hives.

"Do you feel?" And he kept forcing my hand against it.

"Yes."

"What do you think?"

I hesitated in answering and he came forward: "Traces of decapitation, isn't it?"

I shuddered at the tragic word.

"It's the necklace of death, the necklace that holds my life. Feel! Feel!"

And, tilting his head, he walked my hand around his neck, pressing it down and I felt that kind of welt, in erosions and bumps, giving me a frantic shiver in which there was disgust.

Suddenly, pushing my hand away, he rose to his feet.

A burst of laughter roared through the garden and soon afterward Décio's voice:

"Admirable!" And the student appeared, stopped by the bower, blew a kiss to the night and, enraptured, decanted the moon in the suggestive verses of Raimundo Correia:

> *"Star of the mad, sun of insanity,*
>
> *Vacancy, nightly apparition!*
>
> *How many, drinking your effulgence?*
>
> *How many therefore, sun of insanity,*
>
> *Moon of madmen, become lunatics?"*

"I'm going out!" said James abruptly.

"Now?"

"I'm going. You can take the folder, you can take the volume. Goodnight!" And, laying his hand on my shoulder, he gently urged me on. I took the folder and the thick volume and left.

"Goodnight!" I said.

He did not answer. The house slept.

I turned on the gas in my sitting room and, smiling at the memory of that imperious and abrupt farewell, I sat down at the table, untying the ribbons that closed the folder. It was filled with sheets of Whatman paper.

At first, I had the impression of the disorder of that spirit—splattered with ink, full of erasures, of strokes rendering entire paragraphs useless, it was sometimes written in small, fine, straight, stiff characters, sometimes in huge, confused characters, passing, sometimes on top of blots and melts, bending like cornfields to a great wind.

CHAPTER III

That same night I read, or rather excavated, the entire first chapter of the "novel" with slow patience and an effort harder than that of the burrowers after ruins, who dig up the hard bituminous and cobbled soil of dead cities, unearthing antiques.

In addition to the interpretation of the scrawls that took up my time, the slow and difficult unraveling of the seams tangled in squiggles of scribbles, the paragraphs themselves numbered so many and were in such succession that the entire page, latticed with sinuous lines, broke into zigzags between the irregular sentences. It was an intricate web and the eyes were tired following those lines that would, at the margins, cling to the favorite word or phrase like a skein from which they progressed in uncoiled threads.

And yet, creating greater confusion, sometimes the letters curled up in whorls or wrapped up in so many curls that they lost, altogether, their graphic character, making it necessary to guess them.

Figures, linear landscapes were interposed with the terms as childish distractions. Sentences were completed by emblems, like riddles and, not infrequently, large smudges of ink drowned out words truncating prayers, opening veritable chasms after periods.

Even so, I got to the end of the work, not without getting up many times, broken and truly bewildered by what I was painfully extricating by myself from that wall of ideas.

The breeze was refreshing and a sweet light was washing the space, discovering the trees smeared in the shade and the joyful cicadas singing in chorus the festive "alba."

Flights of birds and butterflies announced the dawn and the sun, still cold, cast the first purple. The gas turned livid! I extinguished it.

I leaned out the window. The gardener, seated on the edge of a flower bed, was tying strings for the plants, and the street, in a hustle, woke up to the noise of vehicles. Bells rang, trumpets blared, and the restless leaves of the tall palm trees gleamed golden in the sun.

Alfredo, down below, tousled and barefoot, was throwing buckets of water on the balcony. At the window of his room, despondent and with his hair in a tangle, Basilio was clearing his throat, scratching his sticky gullet.

The scent rising from the garden was pleasant, and the damp earth from the watering exuded freshness.

My eyes burned and my whole limp body sagged into a lukewarm torpor, as if in a fever. The roar of a seashell rang in my ears. I took the *doublet* and went downstairs to recover in a cold bath. I didn't think about a *café au lait*. I threw myself on the bed prostrate without, however, being able to sleep. Outside, the hustle and bustle of life increased with the already tepid light that was breaking.

I let myself stretch out and, enjoying the sheets in sweet slumbering laziness, recapitulated what I had read, the strange content of those tangled pages. Finally, fatigue overcame me and I fell asleep heavily, as if drugged.

I woke up to the ringing of the bell announcing lunch. I dressed, very slow, and went downstairs. Miss Barkley noticed the pallor of my face. I told her I had been up all night.

"Me too," snarled the Commander, picking at his sideburns. "I don't know what was with the Englishman tonight: he paced for hours. It felt like the ceiling was coming down."

"Mister James?"

"Or the devil. What a bad neighbor! And look, Miss, have the gas in my room checked because there's a leak. It reeked all night. The hole must be big. Also, there is no ceiling pipe that can resist the stride of that man. One day the chandelier will fall on my head."

"He left very early today," said Miss Barkley.

"Who?"

"Mister James. He didn't go down to the bath."

"Maybe he's sleeping."

"No, he's not. Alfredo returned with the coffee."

"So he's out and about."

"In Tijuca, for sure."

"He's got relatives there?"

"A Mister Smith."

"That's where he must be."

I went back to my rooms that Alfredo had put in order and flowered, and without losing a moment's rest, I broke some bread, dimmed the light and sat down at the table, opening the green folder. I took two paper notebooks, numbered the pages and in the silence of the house which seemed to be asleep at siesta, I began the translation of the strange manuscript.

#

'The taciturn, grimy house, with thick walls covered in scars that exposed, like the bones of a body, the green slimed stones that were always dripping with a sweat of humidity, loomed imposing among the colossal trees of the park. This background disappeared before my eyes in the dense, dark underbrush of a wood where tall, bushy deer raised bellows to which skittish flocks of wild ducks responded with harsh cawing.

'From the barred, ogival window of my room which opened on the sunset, where I was happy to be entertained for hours and hours, I contemplated the velvety landscape and the calm sky, following the soft undulations of the hills on which white animals grazed. Between the hills a stretch of narrow river that seemed frozen, despite the sun that made it shimmer with the intense brightness of the summer days, and white, very slender, the solitary tower of a church, sharpened like an arrow launching itself from a thicket of chestnut trees around which, every afternoon at the golden hour of sunset, necklaces of swallows swung wide. In the winter the tower, abandoned and stiff against the gray sky, seemed made of snow, shivering in the wind.

'Not a soul appeared before me; only the voices of animals in the distance, or the creaking hoarse call of my ruler, an angular woman, so tall and thin that she bent like a flexible cane, with her copper-colored, black hair escaping in locks, from a coif of silk. She never lost sight of me. During the day she was always following my steps. At night she stretched out on a tiger skin beside my bed, alert and up on her feet at the slightest movement I made.

'If I left my rooms, advancing along the carpeted corridor, I was sure of the spying of her tiny black eyes, sharper than stilettos, which followed me through a crack in a doorway. In time I reached the stairs that, in stages, led to the top floor where Arhat lived. Then the woman, whose name was Dorka, ran to stop me, hideous in her striped silk clothes which gave her the repulsive appearance of a snake.

'Sometimes, in an angry frenzy, grinding her sharp teeth, she would lock me in the room. More than actual chains, it was the power of her magnetic eyes which crippled me, taking away all my energy and my consciousness.

'Only in the mornings and afternoons did she allow me to stay at the window, looking sadly at the distant clouds of the unknown land that my heart yearned for.

'She woke me up early, at the first light of the sun, accompanied me to the bath, helped me to dress and took my morning meal with me.

'Not even during school hours did she leave me on my own.

Huddled in a corner, with her legs crossed, she wouldn't take her sharp eyes off me, while the professors (all shaggy and bald) explained to me the various sciences, taught me different languages, guided in drawing, initiated me in music, or trained me in the handling of weapons.

'Once a week I went up to the great golden hall, where Arhat was waiting for me, always melancholy, surrounded by flowers.

'He was a stunted man of medium height, yellow, emaciated almost to a skeleton but with such dominance from his eyes set in the flower of his face, that I always spoke to him with trembling, even though he welcomed me with sweet affability, caressing me, even relieving my tortured soul from Dorka's nightmare eyes that didn't go beyond his doorway.

'The golden hall, vast and dazzling, gave me the impression of a full sun. The walls, the columns, the great chandelier, the furniture gleamed as if made of light. Yellow carpets covered the floor like a fine luminous grass, and the blue ceiling was truly a summer sky, from which all that dazzling glow seemed to descend in mysterious rays.

'The ambient air was pure perfume, and everywhere, in marvelous abundance, flowers of incomparable beauty were displayed.

'Arhat received me at the door and before bestowing caresses he would look at me with his piercing eyes, take my pulse, and listen to my chest. When the exam was over I would lift myself up by my arms, with a deft strength that none would suspect in such a fragile body, and my day deliciously began with a delicate meal whose origins I never knew. It appeared on a large black lacquer table, covered with a cloth on which the embroideries were in such high relief that the birds and flowers looked more like they perched there, than merely worked into the straw-colored fabric of a metallic luster.

'The crockery, carved in arabesques and with edges of thin filigree, was heavy enough to weigh down the strongest wrist. The delicacies were choice and sober: slivers of cold game layered in diaphanous jams, vegetables, eggs, fruits pulled from the branches themselves, snow, hail and clear water in crystal vases clouded with coldness. Honeycombs in patens, aromatic cakes, dissolving pastilles and an amber liqueur that left my mouth with a violet flavor and enflamed my veins with the vital heat of the sun.

'Arhat watched me eat and, to accompany me, he pecked: a little fruit, a drizzle of honey and as soon as he noticed my satiety, he smiled.

'Suddenly my eyelids were heavy. The impression was instantaneous. I raised them again, but the table had already disappeared and in its place was a bronze incense burner stretched on a column or laying on an ottoman, according to the whim of his prestige that Arhat had chosen to reveal to me once again, burning and smoking with a blue thread. By insistence, I had already become accustomed to this.

'Then we went down through vast deserted halls, courtyards in which truculent statues loomed—a woman with the head of an elephant, a monstrous idol from whose body radiated numerous arms in whose minuscule fists gleamed daggers. We walked through an extensive cloister of laced marble arcades and gained the park.

'Dorka, who was waiting for us below, accompanied us from a distance.

'Oh! the delight of those pleasant hours, free, in the open air, in the sun. I would run along the concave lawns, I would sway on the hammock, between the flowering branches and trees full of nests, or I would get into a boat and sweetly, among swans and water lilies, cross the calm lake under the watchful eye of the governess who uttered guttural cries, thrashing the reeds, if she saw me thrown violently, or would call me to the shore if I jokingly made the boat sway. She would chase me, with the lightness of a *gazelle, when she saw me far away, in the dense shadows of the oak trees where the deer gathered.*

'*How old would I have been then? Seven years, no more.*

'*My desire to know life was intensified. At night, feeling Dorka on vigil by my side, I would remember the words of my teachers, all the notions that, little by little, were filtering into my soul and I imagined the immense world that attracted me with its seas, with its rich and populous empires, with the intense life of its cities, with the sumptuous rites of its religions. Here, green and in bloom, in the warm sunlight; there, barren, silent, shrouded in snow. In one location, fresh and wealthy, thriving in fields of harvest with the quiet joy of the reapers' song; contrasting with the tumultuous bloodied battlefield, blasted and barren in another place.*

'*And I asked myself: "Why the wars? What will happen to the harvest?"*

'*And I envied the wretch who doesn't have a straw roof to warm under in winter, who doesn't find a crust of bread to elude hunger, who doesn't find a rag of wool to cover himself and, thrown into the ditches of the paths, shivers and dies, more despicable than an animal.*

'*Life, true life beyond these ancient walls, this funereal silence, these tomb shadows... was what my spirit asked for!*

'*In that eagerness, repressing instinct, I sadly grew, and was fourteen years old when the first link in the iron chain that held me was broken.*

'*In a bitter December—though in my rooms and throughout the gloomy and desolate house the temperature was invariably the same as on the mild days of spring—the cold was great outside, the weather so harsh that Arhat dared not take me to the park, contenting myself with a few pleasant hours in the greenhouse, among palm trees and tropical orchids.*

'In that harsh December, awake one night, I saw Dorka suddenly rise to her feet, panting, with her left hand flat on her chest.

'His bristled head was struggling anxiously and her hideous face, thinner and more yellow in the lamplight, contracted in grimaces of anguish. A loud snort grated her throat, her bones creaked with continual trepidation, she stretched and drew back her bare and withered legs.

'I was going to get up to help the miserable one, but I felt like I was entangled, tied to the bed, incapable of even turning around: my body was not responding to my will and my eyes, squinting in astonishment, saw more clearly and my ears, which were hyper-aware, listened more finely.

'I reacted in weak impulses and was still struggling in vain when I saw the door open and Arhat appeared wearing a wide silk kimono, followed by a gigantic black man, with a leather breastplate and a short woolen skirt, whose fringes reached to his knees.

'Then the giant bent down, took Dorka's limp body in his mighty arms, and left with the frightened haste of a fleeing thief.

'Arhat sat at the foot of my bed and began to mutter mysterious words, waving his hand in kabbalistic gestures. Then he took a small pan from his belt, rolled a little resin between his fingers, lit it on fire, and started walking around the room with a murmur of prayer, stirring the aroma to spread the lustral smoke intended to purify the room. At last he came to me, laid his hand on my forehead, and left. And soon I freed myself from the force that had held me in afflicted inertia.

'And it was the first time I was afraid. Death had brushed against me, and despite the antipathy that my ruler inspired in me—so strong is the power of habit!—I missed her presence, her squeaky voice, her piercing eyes burning like red-hot iron, her relentless pursuit and her repulsive slim, serpentine appearance.

'I wandered vaguely around the room, astonished, in a daze that made me stagger against the furniture; but sleep surprised me and I barely had time to get to bed before I fell heavily into dream.

'When I awoke in the morning, at the usual time, I saw beside my bed, motionless, two figures that seemed to me of marble, so white and impassive did they stand. But the blue eyes of one, the black eyes of the other, had so much life, the smiles of both were so sweet, the color of their faces so healthy and the gesture with which they greeted me, bowing, were so graceful, that there was no doubt in my mind as to their nature.

'The blue-eyed one wore her blond hair in a long, loose braid, entwined with turquoise strands, a purple bodice high over her buttoned bosom, with a short silk skirt and her slender feet in turned-toed pappuses.

'Gold armillas clasped her toes, and around her plump arms were coiled bracelets from which clinking symbols and amulets hung. Maya was her name.

'The one with the black eyes, a handsome young man, lordly and strong, wore baggy shorts, a lab coat over a fluffy shirt, a belt, and suede boots buckled in silver. On his head, gently tilted and rolled over his jet-black forehead, was a cap, a kind of fez, with a black plume waving gracefully at the side, held in a gold rosette. And he said his name was Siva.

'What then happened to me, only the expression "vexation" can convey. My face burned with shame and no words came to my lips, so disturbed was I in front of those young people who were smiling.

'But the young man spoke and I, who until then had only heard harsh voices, was surprised with ecstasy at the melodious sound with which he announced himself "my servant," humbly asking for the orders of my desire.

'Soon, however, I turned to a soft prelude—it was the girl who repeated her companion's words, and my delighted astonishment remained between the two beautiful smiles, between the caressing lights of those eyes, which seemed to bring a blue spring day, and the blacks, a velvety night of moonlight and dream.

'Oh, the death of Dorka! Dorka's death! It seemed good...

'Feeling ready to leave the bed, the two young people walked away, their footsteps echoing through the chamber.

'Finding myself alone, even though I felt them close, I went to the bathroom where, as usual, everything was waiting for me, from the gushing water to the baths, from the scowling jaws in the marble pool to the lit perfumes misting the room in aroma. In the locker room all the clothes were in order, and I left.

'Once again the castanet sound of the bracelets came to me, preceding the return, already desired, of the blue eyes and the black, and an airy feather waving in the angle of the curtain.

'At mealtime, in the carved oak room, where the dishes were lifted by an elevator, the two flanked me at the table, taking turns serving.

'If he replaced a plate, she, helpful and smiling, would provide the cutlery. He brought the amphora of wine, she offered the cup. If one presented the fruit of my choice, another brought the basket of confections, and the bracelets always sounded and the black plume always waved, airily.

'At the time of my lessons they disappeared. However, when the last teacher left me, they returned, always smiling.

'He held a kind of lyre, whose name—vina—I later learned, was the same as a branch of acacia in bloom.

'As they found me by the ogival window that opened on the west and where I stayed every afternoon, soaking up the *suggestive melancholy of the twilight, they sat nearby, on a rug by Chiraz, and, while the dying sun bled on the hills, marrying to the sound of the instrument, the girl's voice brought to my eyes the first tears I ever cried from my heart.*

'And there the mysterious moonlight found us.'

#

Fatigue won me over. The afternoon was already turning pale with the dread of coming night, when, slumping in my chair exhausted, I stretched out my arms with a wide, unashamed breath. And for a moment I was at rest before rereading the first section of my work.

It did not leave me completely displeased even though at one point or another, for lack of corresponding values in the two languages, I had only extracted the idea by abandoning the expression and, in certain truncated sentences, through forgetfulness or haste or by the frequent smudges that blackened the text, I would complete the thought as I saw fit, always bearing in mind the action and intention of the period.

And I thought about what I had read, about that dream life in an unnamed place, whose vague landscape, sometimes in the sun and sometimes in the mist, could have been that of a romantic province in France or that of a London suburb, an eccentric neighborhood in Berlin or the outskirts of Moscow or mystical Stockholm, azure in the depths of winter.

Yes, it was a dream that asserted itself in the course of the cerebral narrative, increasingly strange, more crazy and more beautiful, full of visuals like a magic opera.

James had wanted to give me a taste of his imagination and had prepared, with subtle ingenuity in the manner of an advertisement, the scene of the salon and that of the delivery, or rather the abandonment, of the manuscript I was translating, not without interest. He might have done the same in the fortunate case that, by the prestige of some benevolent genius, an unpublished tale by Princess Scheherazade had come into my hands.

After a light ablution, I dressed and, leaning out of the window, silently followed the farewells of the end of the day—the slow dissolution of colors, the religious silence of noises, the ecstatic recollection with which Nature makes her intimate evening prayer. I woke up when a sound, coming through space from afar, vibrated joyfully like a festive voice that woke me up.

Stars were already shining.

Again, clearer, the sound vibrated in the silence. It was the bell below. I lit the gas and, looking quickly at myself in the mirror, went downstairs to dinner.

All the guests were at the table, with the exception of James. They didn't even notice his absence. Miss Fanny, always with her eyes lowered, looked paler and sadder, coughing in frequent fits. The butler served attentively under Miss Barkley's eyes.

Pericles, with his napkin stuck in his collar, spoke while beaming: He had revealed an exquisite photographic plate that he had given the title of *Réverie d'une jeune veuve*. A young woman, dressed in black, standing by the waterfall in Parque da Aclamação, her elbow on the back of the rock, her chin crooked in two fingers, staring wildly.

A widow, to be sure, and beautiful... but the attitude, the wavy line of the thin body, the air of rapture!

The tear in her eyes could be guessed. And that dark, scabrous background, with stones bristling with stiff leaves... It was a *true discovery*!

Basilio looked at him sideways, elbowing the Commander, who smiled with his cheeks puffed up by the mashed potatoes. And Pericles, from vegetable soup to guava paste, spoke of photography—of the great advances in art, of a lens he had commissioned, of certain plates of prodigious sensitivity, of the photographic future of the world: all progress contained within the four black walls of a darkroom.

The bookkeeper had listened to him silently, running over a plum with his toothless gums. Finally, snorting the lump and wiping his napkin over his glistening lips, he said:

"It's explained."

They all turned to him, already with a smile on their faces.

"What?" asked Pericles, upright, with an air of suspicion.

"What? The cause of the lack of water in the Campo de Santa Ana waterfall is that the widows go there to cry."

"Now!" pouted Pericles, with a contemptuous gesture.

And that was the "fun" of the afternoon.

Leaving the table, Brandt took my arm and, drawing me to the porch, asked in a mysterious tone:

"Have you seen Miss Fanny? Did you notice?"

"Miss Fanny? What is it?"

"Haven't you noticed her crying?"

"Miss Fanny?!"

"Yes."

"Hysterical!"

"You said it! Never-ending tears. What could it be?"

"You're asking me?"

"Is it for him?"

I shrugged my shoulders. And the conductor pitied her, smiling: "The poor thing!"

Pericles raged through the group, throwing wild gestures, arguing furiously with the Commander and Basilio who were attacking the cinematograph, "a magic lantern with *delirium tremens*."

"Then what is the phonograph? Is the cinematograph life in actuality, but the phonograph just all the mechanical chatter that whines and roars around, thundering through the city? Ah, but against this ignominy you do not rise up, why is that? For photography, my friends, has a guaranteed future. Everything will pass: the book, the newspapers, even the letters, understand? Even the speeches. All documents will be photographed: a firm is falsified, an individual is not. And politicians, instead of wasting words in stupefying speeches, which no one hears or reads, will transmit their ideas through photography, showing there, on the screen, the advantage of their projects, finally exposing their programs live, not baiting the naive people with cute words."

"And instead of saying—'What a great orator!,' one will say: 'What a photographer!'" shouted Basilio and broke into a mocking, grating chuckle.

"And why not? Why not?" lashed out Pericles, already purple. "Why not? It will be the golden age, the century of silence and action. Everything will be done cinematically.

"A thief steals our wallet, a murderer stabs us with a knife, wham! the device prints it out, not only the figure, but also the movements and, in the jury, it is only necessary to unroll the tape and there is the monster projected on the screen of Justice with a sign on his back. And the phonograph?" and he bowed with wide eyes. "*Res non verba* ('Deeds Not Words'), my friends. *Res non verba*, as Cicero said or something like that," he concluded, sponging with a handkerchief the copious sweat from his face.

Crispim, who was furiously picking at his teeth with a toothpick, screeched with a white laugh, sucking the ice shards in the drinks.

Brandt invited me in for some music.

I refused. I felt the need for movement, for action in the open air, for spiritual rest.

Those hours spent in toil, the sleepless night, the worries that the character of that man brought to me, whose life I was beginning to penetrate through the golden and ivory door of an extravagant dream, strained my spirit too much. I left.

The street, with its long colonnade of palm trees like the gallery of a temple, was crossed by strollers all enjoying the freshness. Servants passed collecting their service.

In the shadows of the gardens chirped children and, motionless in the warmth of the arbors, there seemed to be white figures dozing sweetly. In some illuminated houses, pianos played.

I walked slowly towards the avenue. The palm trees rustled nonstop. Trams passed full, in trains of two and three. On the threshold of a door, which opened onto a dark corridor, two men, in shirtsleeves, sat humming, their legs extended.

The broad avenue, almost deserted, with the great pearls of the lamps scattering a pale glow, was silent, as if asleep.

From moment to moment a car would come roaring up, flaming, or it was a slow car that rolled around with the driver stiff, the passengers slumped, silent, disheartened as if they had returned from a funeral.

I leaned against the wall, perching over the sea of lights.

The waves, soft and languid, churned in spurts as in the wake of a ship. But the sky, behind the hills, was little by little serenely clearing as an eventual harbinger of dawn, a curved gleaming thread dropped below the horizon, the chains of the mountains shimmered with snowy light, and the enormous disk of the moon rose with the spectral impassivity of a vision, spreading on the waters its long silver path.

A gulf of fire roared into the horizon. It cooled.

Groups were arriving, attracted by the moonlight: very intimate couples, children at the galleys, and, descending from Botafogo as if in a disputed race, cars, automobiles, and bicycles passed by, lifting a dust cloud that flowed back in rolling waves, dimming the lights, lifting up, and was lost.

A man was approaching with slow steps. He stopped in front of me, slowly uncovered himself, his thin white hair looked wet and his beard, which dripped from his emaciated face in a sour yellow, gleamed with an oily sheen. He looked at me, bowing his head humbly, extending a trembling hand, and muttered a request in which he alluded to his family.

I gave him a coin. He bent over with a hum, waving his hand at me gratefully, and walked away with the same meander, along the wall. A little farther on he turned, stood still for a moment, undecided. Finally, in the isolation of the avenue, he decided to abandon it, looking for rooms, people, souls who would listen to him, who would take pity on his misery.

He looked to the sides, sinking his eyes into the distance and, slowing his steps with an effort and hunched over, crossed the alleys and disappeared in the shadows between piles of bricks, next to the scaffolding of some works: he reappeared ahead, in the light of a lamp and turned the corner.

And I? Where should I go? I felt unable to continue on the tour. My legs buckled and my spirit demanded, in avid curiosity, the continuation of that adventure on which I had started and where I was going, with such rare pleasure, at each period unraveling greater charms, more beautiful wonders, as through branches that moved away in a forest of spells,.

I resolutely took the way home. Upon entering, I thought I saw a figure in the bower, and saluted. Miss Fanny's sweet voice answered from the shadows.

Magnolias were glowing. Brandt played. On the porch Miss Barkley and the Commander, slumped in wicker armchairs, were talking. I stopped for a moment bragging about the night and, as an aside, the commander congratulated me:

"We're free of the Englishman for a while. He wrote to Miss Barkley asking for a few things. He's in Tijuca, with Smith. Will stay there as long as he can."

Miss Barkley, breaking her discretion for the first time, found strange the mystery of that life. It wasn't natural. Many people are eccentrics, but not so many: it was too much. Anyway... Since he didn't bother...

"Does not bother!" exclaimed the Commander. "Except this one. There is no worse neighbor."

"That was one night," I defended. "Of course you weren't sleepy. I share walls with him and I didn't hear anything, even though I was awake."

"Well, yes..."

Brandt's piano notes dominated the discussion. Miss Barkley went to lean against the balustrade, attentive. It was a Listz rhapsody performed with great expression and bravery.

"He plays well!" conceded the Commander.

And Miss Barkley, enraptured, nodded:

"Oh! Very good, indeed!"

And, silent, we listened to the admirable playing.

I went upstairs yawning, ready to go to bed, with brave ideas of work for the next day: I would get up early and, right after showering, resume the translation, taking it until lunchtime and, after a short rest, would advance into the night. But in the sitting room, in front of the table, my curiosity was kindled. I opened the door, slowly leafed through the intricate manuscript and sat down, laying out the paper, taking up my pen and was about to launch the first word when I heard voices, unusual movement below: hurried footsteps, slamming doors, chairs knocked back. I came to the top of the stairs, listened and heard the Commander's voice, who said in alarm:

"Any man of God! Any! There's one right here. But hurry up, boy."

Leaning over, against the mullion, I asked:

"Is there something wrong, Commander?"

The old man, who was close by, went up some steps and, with his hands cupped to his mouth, breathed at me deafly:

"Miss Fanny, the teacher... is bleeding from her mouth. It looks like it's from her lung."

I went down to him. Then, confidentially, he explained:

"We were on the porch when she appeared, coughing in fits and starts... she grabbed a pillar, and when we saw it, it was a gush of blood, perhaps more than a liter, I don't know!"

He scratched his head, his face creased with disgust and horror. "I sent for a doctor. How long have I been saying this? She's a weak creature, to live the life that she does? Slaving, in the sun, in the rain; too much putting up with children? Ambition is behind it. And without a relative, poor thing!"

"And did they give her anything?"

"I don't know! Miss Barkley is brewing a wine potion. She's lost..."

He went down; I accompanied him.

"Do not bother yourself. There's her work there, let it be. Goodnight! Let yourself be."

"But if there's need..."

"No, there isn't."

And he turned around, repeating: "Let yourself be, because she is already in the room and there, you know, not even the sun enters... only the moon, because she is feminine. The doctor won't take long. Good night," and he disappeared down the hall.

I remembered James' mysterious phrase: "Poor lioness!" And for some time I remained leaning against the banister, watching, as if waiting for a new incident, the news of another spurt of blood, the last one, and death to follow. But the house remained silent.

I went up and down the hall, where I felt the light from the gas burner dampen in shivering waves. I raised my eyes: the flame actually retracted as if a mysterious hand were slowly turning the key. Suddenly it went off.

A moonbeam whitened the floor, shattered on the line of the wall. But that light condensed, it all came together in a nimbus as if there were a skylight in the corridor straining, in its disk, the sad pallor of the night. And from the floor it rose in whiteness, growing, taking shape in the shadow.

It formed itself into a slender figure and, under the wide tunic that enveloped it, the soft contours of a female body were outlined. White, as if made of plaster, rigid, in an engraved attitude, it held my eyes and, accentuating the lines of its face, I recognized James' features in them.

His bare arms came out of the soft folds of his tunic, white, reaching out to me with pale hands. It was James Marian, and in that costume his face was more beautiful. It was him, as I had imagined him in my daydream.

Shivering, unable to get myself out of the spot where the darkness had surprised me, I stopped, and cold terror froze me, my mouth dried up, my heart pounded.

But the light reappeared, the gas was re-ignited in a tiny, dubious blue flame, and it grew, like a flower, opening, clearing, and the vision vanished, absorbing itself in the brightness until, again, the corridor appeared illuminated and deserted.

So I was able to walk back. I opened my door, but before entering, in fear of a new appearance, I stopped to examine the interior. Everything was in order. And I breathed as if in salvation from a disaster.

But my legs gave way and I collapsed on the couch, oppressed, breathing in anguish, strangled with fear.

The house seemed animated, expanding, stretching all its stone limbs, all its timbers, swaying on its deep foundations.

Cracking was answered from one piece of furniture to the other, or was it the ceiling boards splitting apart, as if sundering, thundering the dreadful silence with harsh crashes?

Sometimes the light trembled in ways that modified the aspect and position of the shadows, displacing them, and retracting or lengthening them. Inside myself, as if the cold of death were penetrating me, my heart seemed to be knitting together and the blood sometimes drained away, leaving my head hollow. Sometimes it flowed straight to my brain, in a spurt, dazzling me into a full fit of apoplexy.

I got to my feet, measuring the carpet with long strides, avoiding the mirrors with inexplicable fear, but, out of the corner of my eye, I saw my reflection without daring to look at it, certain of finding it changed into the image of another.

I reached the bedroom door, pushed back the curtain—the light came in bands to the edge of the bed, but the background was black, in darkness. And I felt in that darkness something that could not be defined, an impalpable betrayal, the snare of the mysterious invisible.

I returned to the parlor and, resolutely, without even

turning off the gas, took my hat and left.

Still in the corridor, I hesitated before turning the key. Finally, determined, I headed with muffled steps towards the stairs, ashamed of the cowardice of that flight. I crossed the still-lit dining room, the veranda, the garden and threw myself out into the street, aimlessly.

I took the first tram that came down, anxious for the turmoil of life. But the whole city was filled with my terror.

In the dark of the lonely streets they crossed me, gliding through the air! Thin, funereal fluid silhouettes, halos hovering before my eyes and suddenly disappearing. In the crowds themselves, I sensed the presence of a vague, incorporeal being that was integrated among the living, as if to take refuge.

I walked late into the night, making mistakes. I approached the most popular spots, but everywhere, in everything I felt the nefarious influence of a bad aura.

In a hut lost in an alleyway squatted women in bustling groups, their elbows stuck to sordid tables, rolling their glassy eyes languid with drunkenness, smoking, chatting among the throngs of nocturnal rascals to the raucous sound of an accordion that one of them handled.

I stood at the door saturating myself with the exhalation of the concubines, but the vice itself became sinister and the pimps and the harlots, dissolutely accommodated, seemed to me only visions that would dissolve like the smoke that filled the joint. A car drove by with a gleeful roar—two boys and two girls. I took a taxi, ordered him to follow, wanting to cling to that dissipating nonsense. They disembarked at club *Paris*. I entered.

The hall resounded with glee. I sat down at the first free table and, unexpressive, inert and exhausted, I surrendered to the will of the servant who served me supper. Seeing myself in the mirror, I was almost surprised to find myself the same, so changed did I feel inside.

I would stay until dawn in that noise, in the bright light of those chandeliers if the night-people didn't leave. Each expressive in their own way, some singing, stooped-over to girls, their hats on the back of their necks, throwing their legs in dancing moves; others slow, thoughtful, morose, yawning.

I went out, diving into the night that terrified me.

The moon was gone, obscured by thick clouds. A strong wind was blowing.

At a door I thought I could make out Décio's voice in a group.

It was him, all in white denim, angelica in his buttonhole. He spoke of Rodenbach during his outbursts and hyperbole. He saw me and, advancing, truly astonished, his eyes flashed:

"What is this? You! The smoker... at two in the morning, without an umbrella and cloak, on the doorstep of *Paris*! How can this be?! What great changes must threaten this dismal land!" And he approached me, grasped me, examined me to convince himself. "But... can it really be you? What is this?" he asked me secretly, a smile on his boyish face. He took my arm and, with a "Good night!" to the group which was disassembling, he dragged me into the middle of the square. "Come on, give me an account. Pour tonight's adventure into the abyss of my discretion. Tell me about the radiance of her hair, the color of her eyes, the winged grace of her walk. Is she intellectual, does she have a soul or is she a raw Venus, illiterate and lecherous of flesh?"

I told him my fear.

"What! In the house? It's impossible!"

"It is true. I don't know what it was..."

"Perhaps bad wine with dinner?"

"I had none."

"Then, dear sir, you are a sweetheart of the gods, the only man on this graying, exhausted planet who has yet been allowed to enjoy the super-excellence of a *thrill*. Because there are no more *thrills*. The few that remained, Baudelaire consumed. And you've found one! Happy man! And leave the superior feeling to splash in the slime of this infected, Suburran slum! If you promise me a little bit of your fear, a shiver, at least I'll go with you, spend the night by your side. If not, we'll go from there to Copacabana, talk to the old ocean and enjoy a cold beer, which is the dew with which I usually brush the flower of my lyricism, on sentimental nights. Come on, make up your mind!"

I took him with me. He stayed on the divan in the parlor until late, leafing through volumes, thundering the silence with the music of stanzas and bursts of enthusiasm.

CHAPTER IV

I awoke dejected, broken: my whole body ached, and my heavy head was like an immense space full of mists, crossed by the thread of light from a reminiscence far away.

I pulled back the sheets and, lying warmly huddled in the hollow of the bed, my eyes fixed on the ceiling. I began to think about the incident of the night before and as the sun came in through the blinds, illuminating the room, gleaming on the furniture and shining in the mirrors, it seemed I laughed at that "nervousness" that had thrown me out of the house, late at night, into terrified flight.

Then I remembered Decio. I called him insistently. Footsteps rushed into the room and Alfredo pulled aside the curtain, saying, in a surprised tone:

"Mr. Decio? He's been gone for a long time. He took a shower and a cup of coffee and left. Do you want me to bring you your coffee? I brought it before, but you were sleeping."

"Bring it. But tell me: how is Miss Fanny?"

"I think she's improved, yes. But from what I know..." he stretched his lips with a look of dismay and, beating his chest, concluded "it comes from the lungs, consumption. Don't you think so? Look, I scrubbed the porch, I scrubbed it hard because a stain was there. A stain of blood. And later, in the room, she vomited. And the gardener told me that there was also blood in the garden. People, after all, don't have as much blood as there is wine in a vat. What goes out doesn't come back, and it's life itself. So the coffee, yes? Do you want it with milk?"

"No."

"Simple. Very well."

He put the broom down, and ran out.

A useless morning. After lunch, I sat down at the table, opened the folder and spent a long time looking at the dense sheets, crisscrossed with scratches, dotted with stains that complicated even more the interpretation of those intricate doodles.

I got up, went out into the corridor wanting to see the point where the vision had appeared. I carefully examined the floor, the walls, the ceiling, as if looking for a crack through which the fluid body that had appeared before me, in the posture of a statue, halted my step. And there I forgot myself, my spirit lost, my gaze inert, absolutely still in my angry contemplation of the non-existent.

I returned to the sitting room, smiling at my terror, opened the window to the sun, lit a cigarette and, sitting at the table, continued the translation:

#

'From that day on my life changed like a river that, having roiled in anguish into a rough, somber gorge and a bed of mud that bristled with stones, flowed out freely now on a green plain, running between lush trees, under the blue of the sky and the continuous flight of birds and butterflies.

'The hours passed without me perceiving, serenely easy and sweet with the gentle attentions from the companions of my solitude.

'The greatest proof of the charm they were able to create around me was the indifference with which I saw the longed for day arrive when Arhat gestured to me in the splendid golden hall and followed me, patiently, to the park. He allowed me to walk freely in the silent paths, soaking in the light and scents, running on the fine grass, swimming in the lake, climbing up the slopes along the steep foothills, resting among the damp stones, listening to the murmur and singing of the water. I saw up close the skittish grace of the fawn and the lofty bearing of the robust deer, whose branching antlers appeared among the chestnuts like the roots of unearthed trees.

'In all this delight, only one unpleasantness disturbed the sweetness of my life and it came from the sudden shifts which my versatile and indecisive soul struggled, as I was sometimes inclined with more affection to Siva, sometimes devoted entirely to Maya.

'On certain days my heart throbbed eagerly, binding me to the young man, and I rejoiced in intimate pleasure when I felt him close. Just the sound of his footsteps made me excited, happy, and if he spoke I would feel the blood rushing through my veins, my cheeks burning and my eyes, attracted to his, became moist with an influx of tears.

'If the other appeared to me at these times, when my inclination was towards the eyes of black, I would become irascibly irritated and contained with difficulty my impulses of sudden rancor.

'At other times, conversely, the same feeling manifested itself against the airy feather seen so close to the shining hair. It was, then, the maiden that was my delight.

'I wanted her close to me, I took her hands and, burning with a lively ardor, I trembled at the sight of her tiny mouth half open, her swollen bosom, her brief girdle, her fine toes shackled in golden armlets.

'And my pleasure was to be alone with her, silent, my eyes fixed on her face, her hands in mine, or watching her work, smiling, blushing, lowering her eyelids, her breathing quick and panting and roses reddening in her face.

'This sympathy took turns, and always with the same tinge of hatred for what was beyond its reach, as if the heart could not contain two creatures in its affection and feared to lose the one it had chosen for the seductive traits of the other.

'Such inconstancy vexed me and remorse stung me after the rejection of one or the other. So, to get rid of what I thought of as offensive, I relaxed, attributing to my nerves those frenzies that made me act so at odds with my feelings. Always in answer—one or the other—was their smile and, in competition, they redoubled their affection, revealing themselves at my side in the most tender care, attentive to my desires, guessing at them to fulfill them.

'At fifteen I was, in physical development, what I am today—time, completing the man, has added little else to the strength of the adolescent.

'In contrast, however, the soul weakened as the body strengthened. I felt an instinct waning and other inclinations rising.

'The reckless courage of my green years was waning into shyness. The taste for weapons, for exercises in dexterity, for daring moves, faded and the spirit of adventure, which made me yearn for the world with its dangers, was withdrawn. The ideas themselves seemed to take their place.

'Intelligence, formerly so sharp, ready and curious to know, was closed off with repugnance, to certain studies and I preferred flowers to books, exchanged weapons for tapestries and found more interest in seeing them intersect in the fabric of the threads of gold and silk or in the melody of a love song, than in the wise lessons or in the grace of the harnessed rider in which I followed Arhat, a knight as bold and daring as a centaur.

'One night—it was winter and it was snowing—a merry fire burned in the vast marble and bronze stove, spreading a bright purple glow around it. I was reading, sweetly muffled, when all of a sudden I shivered in a harsh shudder as if, behind me, one of the tall windows had been opened and a harsh winter blast fell across my back.

'I turned around, transfixed: all the doors were bolted, no breath had penetrated, the curtains fell immobile in their folds. The cold, however, was intensifying, even though my hands and face kept the heat, natural in that warm environment.

'I brought the armchair closer to the fire and it was as if I had leaned against a block of ice. I smothered myself even more by tugging at my furs and the sensation persisted, unpleasant, morbid, congealing me, making my teeth chatter.

'I wanted to get up and call, but I was paralyzed and I don't know how long I shivered, transfixed, wrapped in furs, looking at the vivid glow of the flame and hearing the crackle of logs.

'It was an internal cold, as if my blood were freezing and my bones had turned to snow. Little by little, however, the heat came and with it a heavy sleep, a sleep of fatigue that prostrated me as if I were dead.

'The next morning I woke up in such a joyful mood, but so stiff, that Maya smiled at my cheer when she came in with an armful of orchids from the greenhouse.

'When I saw her, laying down the sword which she presented to me, I put my arm around her graceful bosom, kissing her twice on the forehead and on the mouth.

'She was not surprised but pleased and, consenting to my delirium, she only lowered her eyelids and her tiny hands were snowy and trembled inside mine.

'What I then felt for that creature, whose name became the engine of my lips, was a true detachment of my being, a submissive surrender of soul, which seemed to have transmigrated into her adored body, from the threads of gold in her hair to the tips of the feet that brought her into contact with the earth.

'I so much wanted to own her shadow, for being the expansion of her body and her part in the light, that I at once gathered all the flowers that perfumed the chamber and my salon, made her stand in the sun while I went covering the shadow, drawing it on the carpet of the chamber. At night, rejecting my bed and like a groom approaching the bride, I lay down on that pillow and passionately fell asleep in my dream of love.

'Listening to her was my pleasure. Seeing her sitting, I knelt at her feet and lost myself staring into her eyes, seeing myself in them again as in the liquid transparency of a lake.

'My greatest joy was feeling her heart, counting the beats and contrasting them with my own. We smiled in such rapture and, sweetly, our heads sought each other, our mouths pressed together: I breathed the breath of her breast, and she received the breath of my chest and, exchanging breath, we lived in the intimate atmosphere where our souls hovered.

'And so, embedded in each other, we managed to forget the time. The night surprised me, and how could I feel it if I had the luminous blue of those eyes and the astral splendor of that golden hair?

'Siva, without ever showing any disrespect for the preference with which I distinguished and fondled his companion, gradually reduced his visits until he limited himself to appearing to me just once, in the morning, pausing on the threshold of the door, mute, immobile, eyes downcast, waiting for orders. He received them and withdrew, and for the rest of the day not even his footsteps sounded nearby.

'And so, in that sweet colloquy, a month slipped by serenely.

'I had become so absorbed in Maya that it was only after such a long time that I noticed that for four instances Arhat had failed to receive me, nor had he even communicated with me. Four weeks without seeing him, the first since my earliest childhood!

'I wasn't deprived of my freedom, which he had granted me on the festive day when he announced to me with fatherly joy that I had turned fifteen, and was able to walk freely in the park and in all the facilities of the manor that were open to me by those who served me. But, I felt uncomfortable and in captivity without the consoling and affable presence of my friend.

'I spoke to Maya, asking for an explanation of that lack that offended and hurt me like an ungrateful abandonment.

'She did not answer. I insisted on cajoling her. She made a gesture with her hand showing space, the beyond, as if to signify that he was gone. And that's all I could get out of her discreet silence. But the next morning I questioned Siva, and the young man, looking at me with his velvet eyes, said:

'"Sir, Arhat shall return in soft days, with the flight of travelling swallows. You will have him with you when the first vines sprout"—and he added nothing else.

'From that moment, inexplicably, my heart began to cool down from the heat in which I was burning. I was already disregarding Maya, deviating from her steps and her so dear voice sounded annoying to me.

'I spent my days recollected in a single thought and, waking at night, I would get up barefoot and lightly, barely touching the carpet, I would go to the door, open it over the extensive gallery lit by opaque lamps that looked like lilies and magnolias between the foliage of the carvings. I let myself look with an intense desire to go up that staircase that wound up at the bottom, reach the hall, open a tiny door, a kind of antechamber, from which at times Arhat emerged. His quarters must be beyond there.

'But the fear that I would be caught in such indiscreet wantonness, of incurring the displeasure of the almighty man, held me back.

'Late one night, however, when the wind was blowing furiously and the snow was thick—the whole house was asleep—I got up and decided, and went out into the gallery with unshakable resolution.

'My footsteps crackled on the carpet like green wood on the fire, I was trembling all over, even though I wore a fur cloak over my shoulders. I walked. In front of the stairs I stopped still.

'The lamps cast a snowy light across the staircase, the mullions gleamed in swirls of silver, and above, in the circular opening, the brightness seemed brighter, like a skylight in full sun.

'I climbed fearfully and my knees buckled in violent tremors.

'I reached the top and my courage, which had slackened, rekindled more fiercely, urging me toward the gleaming marble foyer which a bronze chandelier illuminated with daytime splendor.

'There was the door to the hall with the capricious reliefs, in profuse promiscuity, of a most complicated sculpture of monsters and tragic gods. I walked. The doubt still assailed me: How to open it? But before each door, touching it only lightly, I felt it move, slide, turning sweetly on the hinges, leaving me free passage into the hall that blazed with a blinding splendor of fire.

'The columns were flaming cylinders, gleaming, radiating with the fiery glow of the flaming logs; the frames glowed. The floor, covered by the fiery-colored carpet, looked as if it had been curdled with combustible lava. And there rose in waves, warm and dizzying, thick smoke which permeated the atmosphere with the scent of spices.

'Countless tall censers exhaled blue whorls—on bizarre tripods, on shallow pedestals or settled on claws.

'A bronze pyre burned in the middle of the hall, flaming azure, now in a single, pyramidal flame, now in split tongues that flickered.

'I shuddered suddenly. Someone followed me, stalked me. I fell, terrified in my heart, muffled, breathless. I looked and then I recognized in my silent pursuer my own image—not one, as at first it had seemed to me: many, reproducing themselves in all the mirrors that faced each other, widening, deepening the hall *indefinitely, multiplying the golden columns, the tripods, the lit pyre, the furniture and my image that in a long line repeated, with mechanical isochronism, all my movements.*

'*I ventured to the hidden door, wedged in an arched recess. I pushed it; it gave way without a sound, opening onto a sort of crypt with an odorous and bluish atmosphere from the vaulted ceiling of which hung a lamp in the form of a shell with shimmering pale flames rising from seven spouts that radiated outwards. My feet sank softly, softly, into the thin fluff carpet; and so thick was the air that I moved through it, conquering it, with the effort of a swimmer breaking a wave.*

'*The glow of a furnace spot-lit the end of the passage in flames. I rushed through it, almost running, and came out in a circular enclosure like the inside of a dome filled with a funereal, mourning, purple light, filtering through porcelain ampoules.*

'*In the walls, lined with violet silk, embroidered with silver lilies, strange niches were dug, jagged like caves, guarding idols with blazing eyes.*

'*A huge golden lamppost hung at the center, suspended by a serpent with gleaming scales. In equally spaced bronze cups aromatic resins crackled, and bunches of flowers faded in large onyx and alabaster urns. On a low bed, at the head of which a Buddha of human proportions sat, was a body covered by a very thin, diaphanous and subtle veil.*

'*I lifted one end slightly and it billowed out, rippling like mist in the wind.*

'*I uncovered the whole body and recoiled in horror with a violent tremor, recognizing, in the corpse that lay there, Arhat.*

'*The funereal light filled his pale, sunken face, turned his shriveled hands purple, sunk into his eye sockets, set his sharp chin more protruding.*

'*Terror overwhelmed me—my spirit was gone and my*

body surrendered, slumping beside the bier.

'I hesitated, my knees bent in cowardly lassitude. I leaned against an urn.

'Dark noises rumbled, maybe the wind moaning outside or... who knows! I got up and groped uncertainly, no longer perceiving the tomb glare of that precinct of death, I walked stiffly, stiffly, bumping into the walls and, reaching the vaulted passage, I started running in terror.

'Going out to the hall, my eyes were blinded by the intense light. I gained the vestibule, threw myself on the stairs in a vertiginous flight, and crossed the gallery.

'When I reached my rooms, I stretched out my arms, throwing myself against the door as if to burst it open.

'Behind the open door and in the middle of the chamber, in broad, sinister light, Arhat was standing, staring, motionless.'

#

The afternoon was turning pale when I suspended work, stretching out on the couch and resting. My interest in the manuscript, far from growing with the curious development that the "novel" was taking, descended into simple literary interest. It was not, as I had assumed, a true study, but a fantasy, pure fiction woven with some ingenuity onto a dazzling canvas.

The Englishman had amused himself at my expense by offering me his literature in a cloak of mystery.

In short, it was a distraction for my empty hours and, if it didn't put me on the threshold of the arcane, it showed me in full light the radiant imagination of a romantic.

It got dark. The cicadas sang in concert. Suddenly I felt a jolt as if the house had been suspended on its foundations, and then a rumbling was followed by a violent crash, another, another...

It was from the nearby quarry, the formidable explosions near the mines, displacing blocks of stone from the sides of the mountain, veritable cliffs which rolled down noisily, often bringing with them coconut palms, old trees, crusts of earth covered with weeds, crushing them all against the edges of the monstrous scalloped rock.

I got dressed and the shadows were already thickening in the corners when I turned on the gas and went down to dinner.

The bright room, with the chairs around the flowered table and covered in glittering china and crystal, was still deserted. Guests were beginning to appear on the porch, walking through the garden.

Brandt, always alone, enraptured in his dreams, listened intimately to the ancient rhythms, the soft expressions of dead melodies. He came and went slowly, along the cool alleys, turning around the wet beds of water brushed by the young roses that leaned languidly on the stems, already under the effluvia of the nocturnal voluptuousness.

Sometimes he would stop, reach out to a branch, take a leaf between his fingers and roll it, crush it with eyes lost in the heavens, absorbed as if after a dream that was sweetly diluted in the ether and had vanished, merged with the night, between dreams.

Basilio, huddled in a straw chair, was poking around, with nosy eyes, for something on which to hone his sarcasm. Carlos and Eduardo, together, at the balustrade, were whispering. Crispim was whistling softly, leaning against the threshold of one of the doors.

The house had a melancholy air, something gloomy hovered over its expression of joy. It's appearance was different: demolished, dejected, as if in fatigue.

The Commander and Pericles appeared. Basilio, noticing them, turned around in his chair:

"Well? How did it go?"

"Badly," said the Commander.

"Oh, this illness! And the doctor?"

The old man shrugged. Curiosity gathered all the guests into a group and the bookkeeper, staring at Pericles:

"Did you go to see her?"

"No," said the other, flinching. "Penalva understands. I do not. What am I going to do there?"

"A snapshot, man. The scene lends itself..."

"Nonsense!" grumbled Pericles, turning his back on him.

The bell vibrated. We entered. Miss Barkley appeared unchanged, nodded and took her place. The servant came in with the tureen and, in silence, with the respect of a rite, dinner began.

Penalva had a more serious manner, the composure of a man full of responsibilities. It was known that the doctor had asked him for help, entrusting the sick woman to him, making him the depository of that life that he felt was slowly extinguishing, despite the efforts he made to keep it in that weakened and fragile body.

"So, doctor?" asked Basilio. "Miss Fanny?"

The student grimaced.

Brandt stared at him.

"Have you no hope?"

"Hope? It's lost," he concluded, putting a crust of bread in his mouth.

Miss Barkley drew in a longer breath and, reaching out, arranged some roses in the vase.

"What strikes me are the hallucinations."

"Hallucinations!" exclaimed the Commander.

"Yes, hallucinations," Penalva insisted.

Brandt's eyes widened and lit up.

"Hallucinations?" he asked.

"Truly. Last night, as soon as the doctor left, the hallucinatory state began to manifest itself. She was lying peacefully, seeming to be asleep, when suddenly, shuddering, she sprang to her feet, sat up, eyes wide, staring at the back of the room. We tried to lay her down, she gently pushed us away, remaining in the same ecstatic attitude, very pale, all cold, trembling. She stayed like that for a moment until, hiding her face with her hands, she broke into sobs, letting herself fall on the bed as if abandoned."

"It was Mr. James," said Miss Barkley.

There was an uproar at the table, and many voices exclaimed with surprise:

"Mister James?!"

"Yes," said the Englishwoman serenely.

Everyone then put down their cutlery and bent to listen to her, slowly taking in her words and, in the anxious silence, she continued after a pause:

"Yes, Mister James. That's what she told me. She saw him at the head of the table, not he himself, the man, but a girl who had his face, robed like a statue."

At the Englishwoman's words, a shiver ran down my spine, my hair stood on end, all my skin twitched with an irritating itching.

"Poor thing!" concluded Miss Barkley.

Looks were exchanged and dinner went on in silence. Basilio, however, erupted in a tone of derision:

"So... in a tunic? A women...?"

Miss Barkley nodded in affirmation.

"Well, look, she hasn't discovered something previously unknown. I, despite not having seen him in a tunic like a statue, have always classified him in the other sex."

Miss Barkley glared.

"Sorry, Miss, but it's the truth."

Violently pulling the napkin from his collar, he exclaimed: "Well, is that a man's face?!" And he spread his gaze around, consulting his listeners. "If we had police I guarantee that this case would already be solved. Because, after all, who here knows?! Russia is full of anarchist women, and they are worse than men. Anyway... the best thing is to shut up. Let them come!"

He attacked the roast beef, lunging with savage fury at the piece of meat that bloodied his plate, already stuffed with lettuce.

Brandt looked at him with contempt, pecking with slow and distracted bites, not saying a word until the end of dinner. Sometimes the corners of his mouth curled up with the fleeting trace of a smile.

Basilio lashed out, indignantly, against James' beauty, with the scandalized revolt of a Puritan in the face of obscene turpitude.

As we rose, Brandt, taking me by the arm, asked in a confiding tone:

"Do you have to stay?"

"No."

"Come with me. This man irritates me and tortures my nerves."

And he turned to glance at the bookkeeper, who dominated

the porch, raging with hatred.

We left. The musician, as we walked to the chalet, kept silent, torturing his thin mustache.

The room was dark and stuffy. Brandt opened the windows wide. There was a wide flutter of curtains in the wind.

In the glow of the gas, the entire artistic ensemble of the interior emerged from the shadows—varnishes and blades flashed, the flowers shimmered in the light, the canvases, in wide frames of gold and lacquer or of waxed wood, showed distant horizons of meadows, vivacious little flowers, still waters, woods and cattle. The sad storks, on the screen, in a glitter of gold and silk threads, seemed to ruffle their feathers. Brandt leaned against the piano and, with a cigarette between his fingers, swinging his leg, looked thoughtful. I sank into the armchair, smoking. A damp, gusty wind shook the flowerless jasmine branches.

The sad night, dark and warm, hung like an cavern.

"My dear man," said the musician, "extraordinary things are happening in this house. Truly prodigious things."

"Why do you say that?"

"Did you hear what Miss Barkley said about Miss Fanny's vision?"

"Yes. That it was James..."

"Well, my friend, I am not ill, nor will anyone say that I have been impressed by this or that, because I only found out about the teacher's illness this morning. Last night, however, perhaps near one o'clock, finishing my study I leaned out of the window, distractedly looking around, and saw a figure appear on the veranda, pause for a moment, slowly descend the stairs, cross the lane of acacia trees to the jasmine arcade where he remained motionless. He was dressed exactly in a white, diaphanous robe, on which, at times, a ray of cerulean light was projected. I thought at first that it was the teacher, even though the outfit seemed extravagant to me, so to convince myself I went out into the garden. The figure remained in the same position. I rushed forward, and at a distance of about ten paces, I felt as if I was enveloped in snow, frozen. I stopped, staring and recognized in the lights...

"James."

Brandt nodded, confirming it: "James."

"And then?"

"The jasmine tree was coated with whiteness, like a mysterious moonlight emitting only for him, but the pallor stood out, undulating, and then rose into the light air, tenuously fading. It hovered, for an instant, over the arch, retracting, expanding, ascending gently, then swiftly, as if carried by a strong wind, then it disappeared... I saw it!"

He lit the cigarette, sat down on the piano bench, his gaze vacant, lost.

"Well, my dear Frederick, the same thing happened to me. I would have said nothing if you had not communicated your vision to me. The same thing happened to me at almost the same time."

And I described the apparition that had appeared to me in the darkness of the corridor.

"And what do you say to that?"

"I? I don't know. Don't you believe in collective hallucination?"

"I neither believe nor doubt: life is a mystery and I live. This Englishwoman, with whom I have always sympathized because I felt her unhappy, is one of those spirits of love who only live to love. Withdrawn in virtue, she expands in goodness. Like a virgin tree covered with flowers, sterilizing itself in perfumes. The fruit is from the earth, the perfume is from space. Apparently it is an inert force, but... The rose is a fragility, a nucleus of shells whose pearl is the aroma... And the rose poisons and kills, like love. Miss Fanny is on the path, enslaved to James and as for him, who knows? This apparition coinciding with the Englishwoman's illness..."

"So, is it he?"

"Who else?"

"But in that case, he must be dead..."

"Because?"

"Because only the dead appear."

"But the spirit is immortal, my friend. As Thought is its restraint, Will is its Strength. Anyone who could concentrate so much that he was absorbed in himself would immortalize matter, impregnating it with eternity. The acts that we call unconscious are products of the creative *mens*, energy that does not lie subordinated to matter, like intelligence, but surrounds it, circulates around it like a sun.

"The brain is a lamp and intelligence is a wick—the fire that ignites it is inspiration, the *mens* I alluded to, is the very essence of life and this essence, so often repudiated when it manifests itself inopportunely, is what we call an idea. If our eyes were not prepared exclusively for material vision, we would see the environment and understand the Truth and all the false notions that stun us, starting with that vacuum we call Time, would disappear like specters that the sun scatters.

"The dead do not manifest. What we call dead is the corpse— spoiled. A tunic is not put on straight but adjusted to a body. When matter is contained in sleep, the spirit can leave without life failing to sustain it with its dynamics.

"Consider a barge to the port, rig the boatman to sail, secure the oars, remove the rudder, tie it up and jump ashore. In the heaving wave, the boat continues to hum. If the cable that holds it tight breaks, it moves away, crashes or capsizes, but if it doesn't break the line and escape the shelter, it stays until the owner returns, who climbs on the deck again and heads for the open sea.

"Life is the sea, the boat is the body, the boatman is the soul."

"Remember *Genesis*? There it is, in the second couplet: '*The spirit of God moved over the face of the waters.*' It was the Absolute Soul, the Eternal Fecundity hovering generatively over the still motionless ocean of universal life. Jesus lived among fishermen—souls. What is the storm of Lake Tiberias but the representation of the storms of Life? And did not Christ, despising the boat, walk on water in the sight of the disciples? Because? To what end? To show that the spirit of God is not without a body.

#

For a long time we sat in the silence of our thoughts. Brandt stood in front of me and, with blazing eyes, whispered to me as if he were afraid of being overheard: "My dear man, Science is a spiral column, always turning. It seems to us that the scrolls advance, climbing to heights... unfortunately this is just an illusion, pure illusion, isn't it? We reach the cornice of the Temple, from there up is the great void and the spirals auger, auger...

"We talk about progress and we turn into death. Nothing is known. If I consider music to be the most spiritual of the arts, it is because music is pure essence. Rhythm is its law, its manifestation is the sound of nature, light and ether, simple vibration, ethereal wave, nothing more. Music explains the invisible to me, in a way, and I understand the soul when I perform, I feel God when I compose."

"You?"

'Yes, me. All artists descend from the ideal to the real, the musician ascends; from the real to the ideal. Poetry compresses Thought into words, sculpture is of stone or metal, architecture is mortar, painting is paint—music is rhythm and it is sound: the indefinite.

"Sound is like the smoke of censers—a winged prayer.

"In the temples, in primitive times, the lyres resounded near the censers and the waves, twinned, rose in the same flight—those of aroma, in cloud; the sonorous in melody. A poem is what it is—a stratification of ideas: the statue is a copy of life at a standstill; the building, a set of inflexible lines; painting is the vision of a point in space in the light of a rays of the sun. Singing is breath, soul, and, being soul, it is essence.

"Life is a rhythm that unfolds in rhythms as the wave multiplies in ripples."

#

Gesturing with his hand at random, he struck a note on the piano—the sound vibrated, resounded, faded, and died out.

He raised his arm and, with a stiff finger, made a terrifying gesture, muttering: "The spiral... The spiral..."

He walked to the window and was silent for a moment, his eyes plunging into the darkness outside. But soon, turning, he continued:

"That apparition didn't frighten me, it just shook me like an uttered truth. It was a flash of lightning that made me glimpse the beyond. But let's stay with music. You said a few days ago, speaking of Beethoven, that you found him admirable, but that you didn't understand him."

"Yes. Many of his symphonies' proclaimed beauties go, by me, unnoticed."

"It's natural. Imagine that you arrived in a theocratic country and immediately entered the temple where the most solemn ceremony of religion was celebrated in all magnificence.

You would see the interior of the majestic building, splendid in its marble, gold and gemstones; you would see colossal idols on sumptuous altars; you would see the resplendent priests silently describing mysterious developments; you would see the virgin priestesses dancing to the sound of bronze sistrums; you would hear the deprecation of the mob and you would be dazzled, certainly, but you would not feel the mystical emotion, for not understanding the terms of the prayer, the representation of the dances, the value of the attributes, in short, the rite. However, as you began to be introduced to esoteric symbols, that is, to the "intimate reason" of the ceremonial, your enlightened spirit would apprehend the beauty and significance of the most subtle passes and you would attain the ideal truth. Music is like that.

"It is not enough to hear it, it is necessary to understand it, feel it, interpret it: to have the emotion and the knowledge. In Beethoven's symphonies there is not an excessive note as there is not a useless leaf in the most verdant tree.

"Music is an apparently easy language, but it is the most difficult of all. There are seven notes, some in the lines, as if thrown on the earth, others in space, hovering: reptiles and birds, carpet and cloud, flower and star. Seven are the values, seven the rests, seven the accidentals, seven the clefs, three the measures. It's little and it's everything. All voices, all noises fit on the agenda. The chords are five and enough: on them the subtle breeze hums and the fury of the storms rumbles loudly.

"All the harmonies of nature are contained within the fence of the pentagram."

#

He stood looking at the window, soaked in silence.

The jasmine branch swayed slightly as if beckoning him, reaching out to touch him.

A moth fluttered around the gas lily. Brandt didn't make the

81

slightest movement, absorbed, dreaming, frozen in thought as if on the edge of an abyss.

"What are you pondering, Frederick?" I asked worriedly and he, as if surprised, turned around, his eyes clouded over, pale, and putting his hand to his forehead, ruffling his hair, muttered vaguely:

"I do not know, I do not know..."

He opened the piano, sat down and, with his hands flat on the keyboard, he performed ecstatically. Suddenly, he got up, began to walk along the room, head down, and repeated in a muffled voice: "I don't know." He planted himself in front of me, his gaze fixed, annoyed:

"I look crazy, don't I? If you could only imagine what I feel... The music overwhelms me. Wagner was right—*'it is literally the revelation of another world.'* And I feel so much, so intensely! Inspiration comes to me in turmoil, but it happens that the ideas, because they are many, run over each other and stay like an excited swarm that wanted to enter, *en masse*, through the narrow entrance of the hive. It's horrible! You can't imagine. Excess fertility is like the flooding of rivers, it is like the plethora in the veins—it subverts, it suffocates."

At that moment a bust appeared at the window, pushing the jasmine branch away, and both Brandt and I were thrilled with the same amazement. It was Penalva. The fifth year, noticing our disturbance, looked at us confused:

"Was I indiscreet?"

"No. Come in. We were talking."

He apologized:

"I was at Miss Fanny's bedside. I was just passing on a request from the sick woman."

"A request? And how is she?"

82

"Bad. Another hemoptysis."

Brandt urged him to come in. It was drizzling.

Brandt opened the door. The student acceded, without however accepting the armchair that the musician indicated. "No. I can't linger." And then, with a vexed smile:

"She sends me to ask you for some music on the harmonium."

Brandt's eyes gleamed and a livid pallor covered his face.

"Poor thing!" He moaned with emotion and opened the harmonium, passing a handkerchief across the keyboard.

He flung open the windows and door so that the sound passed in free waves. Penalva went out and, on the threshold, leaning back in, said:

"Goodnight!"

"Why hurry, man!"

"She's in a bad way, maybe she won't make it to dawn. Miss Barkley is there, but... see you tomorrow..." and he threw himself into the lane, running.

The harmonium sharpened to the pressure of the pedals operated by Brandt.

"And so?!" exclaimed the musician, nodding inquiringly.

"What?"

"This request. What do you think?"

"Romanticism."

He smiled and, bending over the instrument, soon a very soft sound developed into a phrase of suggestive melody, and he said, with upturned eyes:

"Music, my friend, is a religion for those who feel it."

"What is this you're playing?" I asked delightedly.

"The *Theme of the Fatal Passion*, from *Tristan & Isolde*." He broke off and, taking an album, flipped through it, opened it on the shelf and announced: "Bach's *'Prelude in E-flat Minor'*. Worth all of *Genesis*, old man. Listen. It's all a creation."

He sat down for a moment, his head back, his eyes fixed. Fingers on the keyboard, he attacked the first chord.

There was a thunderous melee in the foliage outside, a flurry of rustling branches. Windows slammed in a fiery gust. Lightning flashed shiveringly.

But the low sounds rose like a prayer in the night. In the distance, sullen thunder rumbled and the broad sentences, of a virgin nature, unfolded, grew long and the impression they produced in my spirit was that of a chorus of painful voices that mysteriously intoned in the dark spaces.

Howls of the wind continued through the night, from moment to moment, lapped by a stroke of lightning. Suddenly the musician froze, stood up nervously, glancing around.

"What is it?"

The rain thickened, rustling the leaves, showering on the walls. Brandt reached the window, moved the jasmine branch, was about to close the blind, but hesitated. Again the loose branch swung across the room, swaying, and the musician returned to the harmonium.

"Why don't you close the window?"

He shook his head in the negative and, through divine music, said as if speaking in a dream:

"What does it matter! It was, perhaps, to help her fall asleep that she asked me to play."

And, overcoming the raucous torrential rain, the harmonium sounds, sometimes painful, filled the night with human anguish.

CHAPTER V

Despite Brandt's insistence that I stay, I braved the raging storm and retreated to my quarters with all my clothes soaked and my feet in puddles. Until late, through rumbles of thunder which seemed to explode over the roof, the rain poured down.

In the dark of the room, where the lightning, insinuating itself through the cracks, lit up the vases in a blaze, the perennial and lulling sound of the water running and the stiff battering of the wind, increased the violence and the shudder was pleasant.

I fell asleep sweetly enjoying the soft covers of my bed, the safe protection of my rafters.

In the morning, going down to the bath, right on the stairs I heard the news of Miss Fanny's death. Pericles, who was dressed in a nightshirt, his hair ruffled and holding a soap dish and sponge, asked sadly:

"Do you know?" And, in response to my astonished muteness, he announced: "The Englishwoman... Gone! At five in the morning."

A pang of anguish rose in my throat. I didn't say a word. We looked at each other and Pericles, frowning and shaking his head in desolation, picked up his nightshirt, showing his thin hairy legs, and went slowly up the stairs, muttering regrets.

Basilio was already ready in the dining room with a waterproof that hung down to his feet, drinking coffee at the table. Seeing me, he widened his hooded eyes and, throwing the last sip down his throat, came forward, stepping softly in wellies, to whisper to me with an air of triumph:

"So? What did I say?" But sulking, his face all corrugated, he said bitterly: "Now it's time to wait for the consequences. We'll have them here, from Public health. It won't be long until they're here, with their acids and infernal stoves. It will be a calamity! At the time of the bubonic outbreak, the so-called *rat bubonica*,"—and he rubbed his fingers in the meaning of thievery—"I lived on Rua de S. José. A guy died there, they thought he was a pest... Well, my dear, those guys from Saúde ran inspection of the house and I don't need to tell you! I didn't have a pair of underwear to change. Now imagine! I have a new frock coat, which I haven't put on yet. You, meanwhile... It's not for lack of charity, but these events in a house like this, full of people... Hospitals are for dogs. I tell you: if I get sick, send me to my Order. I have everything there on time, I'm at ease and I don't owe any favors. And then what... consumption! Where it enters, it stays, it's like the bed bug. I do all this because I don't have time, otherwise I would move. Are you going to the funeral?"

"I don't know."

Basilio clicked his tongue against the roof of his mouth:

"Don't go, man. Religion is different. I won't go. I don't go into cemeteries, too many foreigners. Not for nothing, it's just a matter of principle. That's not for the living. I will go when they take me, but I won't walk there. Neither to masses, nor to cemeteries."

As he spoke, planting his foot on the edge of a chair, he was folding up the hem of his pants. He picked up his umbrella, shook it and, with an air of disgust, exclaimed: "Bloody weather!"—He lit a cigarette and, lifting the collar of the waterproof, left on tiptoe, softly, wary, afraid that he would be called to something.

Coming back from the bathroom, crossing the walkway, I saw Brandt, still in his pajamas, at the door of the chalet, gazing thoughtfully at the trees drenched by the rain, dripping in a sadness of humble weeping.

Seeing me, he stretched out his arms, throwing them in the air in a great gesture of consternation. He stepped out onto the threshold and, squinting, with the rain spraying his face, asked:

"Are you going to the funeral?"

"I don't know. And you?"

He recoiled with the wind that pushed the rain through the door and, from the middle of the room, shouted loudly:

"It's difficult. I have a lesson today in Niterói. Anyway... I could be there. What time will it be?"

"At four, of course."

He thought for a moment, twisting a lock of hair that curled on his forehead. He finally made up his mind, resolutely:

"I'm going. We should both go. We'll take a car together. See you later."

#

At lunch Miss Barkley gave the obituary of the deceased, describing her virtuous life, from the day she had come here aboard the *Danube* until that sad morning.

She was from a Puritan family in Scotland. Her father had been a professor at Oxford, and she, the youngest of eight children who had dispersed, had grown up always scrawny and limp, amidst sullen sages and iron-stern Quakers, moving from scientific controversies to shrewd commentary on the Bible, among the choir of Luther and the sweet songs of the highlanders. At night, recalling the native land in an upper room, these old men and friends of the house, gathered at the table or around the fire, sang in mystical tones, as if invoking the hill deities and offering them, in their nostalgic song, the sacrifice of another day spent in the land of exile.

She had educated herself solidly, and at the age of eighteen, had left her parental home for Australia as a governess. For three years she had lived there and then, in need of sunshine, she had come to Brazil where, in a glow of incessant work, she had managed to establish an honest name, and was always found in a halo of children who stunned her heart's longing and her soul's thoughts with the festive noise of their toys and the clear joy of their laughter. A valuable girl! Very valuable!

Penalva, who had not left Miss Fanny's bedside for a minute, said of her death with compassion: "She joined her hands, and closed her eyes as if to sleep. Not a tremor, not a sigh. She was dead."

The Commander took a deep breath and snorted with feeling:

"Poor girl!"

The servant served the steak in silence. A bell toll rolled melancholy and velvety in the misty air, and the clock began to chime vibrantly, announcing the time in a merry tone.

There was a scrape of feet on the porch, the clatter of umbrellas being closed, the murmur of whispered voices, and at the door of the room, as on a school party day, a group of blond children in white appeared, their eyes amazed and curious, all with bunches of flowers.

Miss Barkley rose to receive them. They were followed by maids in aprons and bonnets, very serious, their air somber.

They entered with muffled steps, leading the dappled children.

A scent of flowers wafted sweetly through the air as if carried on orchard breath, and the flock slipped in a line, disappearing into the tiny mortuary room.

The Commander confessed that he was truly sorry for the "catastrophe."

"So young! Poor thing..."

Penalva asked if he had already gone to see her. The old man spread his hand before his eyes as if in revulsion at a terrifying sight, with his whole face in a disgusted grimace:

"No. I don't like to see dead people, they are always

impressive and people, when they reach a certain age, should avoid these spectacles. If a rainy day like today makes me nervous, imagine a dead creature. No! I want myself with the sun, with the noise, with life."

And he bent over the coffee cup, sucking on it.

Penalva referred to the beauty of the deceased:

"She looks like marble, Commander, even her freckles have faded. She's beautiful!"—the old man looked at him with widened eyes and the student said—"Yes, sir: beautiful! There are women like that, as if they were made for the grave: ugly in life, beautiful in death. There was a case like that at the School... A certain girl of the world, during her illness in the hospital, was hideous, disgusting. Hours after her death, it was as if a scaly crust had been peeled off her face, revealing the pale, thin skin of fifteen, she surprised everyone with her beauty. People gathered in the amphitheater to see her. Décio sang her a sonnet, a beautiful sonnet!"

"No!" the Commander snapped, in disbelief.

"I assure you!" confirmed Penalva, very seriously.

"Well, my friend, in any case, I prefer life."

We got up and, each one going to his room, the house was silent, in the veiled light of the dismal day, under the misting of the drizzle that spread in the air in a fluttering spray, like a cloud of mosquitoes over a vast marsh.

#

The day was warm and sullen. At times, through an open slit in the clouds, the sun gleamed dully, sickly, filtering a yellow candlelight. Soft thunder rolled lazily in the distance and the flies, invading the muffled interior, fluttered impertinently and chased each other in a lewd fury, with a monotonous buzz that made the warm and sultry silence even more attenuated.

I tried to work, but my attention turned to the dead woman's chamber.

A breath of aroma invaded the room as if it had risen from that funeral room, and then I felt I saw the Englishwoman's corpse, pale, as Penalva had described to me, framed in white roses and lilies, her hands rigidly clasped as in the fervor of a prayer, a blessed smile stamped on her face.

I opened at random the thick mysterious volume that James had lent me and began to look at the cryptographic squiggles that filled it: reversed lines, disks, spirals, urn shapes, crescents set on double-crossed crosses, magical signs, silhouettes of animals as in hieroglyphics. And, leafing through it vaguely, absently, I came to the last page in which an illumination was blooming—a green stem from which an airy lily Hung plumb and another hung limp and weak, just as on the frontispiece.

There was no doubt—it was a symbol enclosing all the mystery of that twisted script.

My eyes clung to the bizarre figures, and whether it was an illusion of fatigue or a marvelous truth, all the characters began to move slowly—the spirals unrolled, widened like stupefied snakes that were being revived in a gentle heat; the discs bulged, grew into globes and rose from the pages like iridescent soap bubbles; the urns stood up; the crescents lit with a pale moonlight on the black crosses that spread out their inflexible arms to and fro; the various signs whirled in a vertiginous spin, and the animals, growing, gaining weight, bent their backs, spread their wings with their hair or their feathers ruffled and their eyes flashing, fierce in combat and fleeing the stars or shaking in flight, terrified, dissolving like halos of smoke that vanish into the air. I rubbed my stunned eyes for a long time. Returning, then, to the page, I reviewed everything in its primitive and natural fixity. Illusion!

I started to walk around the room, repelling the dark thoughts that followed me.

Why should that dogged idea of death trouble my mind? The corpse, which I felt was suspended above me, hovering, stiff and cold, white, among flowers—why should it follow me?

I looked around, clear-eyed, and I saw nothing, nothing! However the dead woman was still with me, involved me, obsessed me.

In the steely glow of the mirrors there were, at times, obstructions, mists that obscured it as they passed, but soon the light would reappear brilliantly.

It was nothing but the reflection of the sky, sometimes shadowed, sometimes clarified by the indecisive sun.

I threw myself on the bed, prostrate, always thinking about that trance at dawn, that soul that had left the earth and suffering for the bosom of the mystery. I wanted to follow her, to see her resolve into light, to blend in with the infinite clarity while I looked straight at her. Feeling sleepy, however, I tried to get up to call Alfredo and put him in charge of calling for a hearse, but the lassitude was such that I could barely get up, and then I fell back on the pillows, falling asleep immediately.

An icy hand touched my forehead lightly, squeezed my own hand that hung on the edge of the bed, and, opening my eyes in fear, I saw a wintery form, a subtle, diaphanous body, undulating like a reflection of mist in shivering waters, emerging and flowing in silent succor.

I sat up suddenly, stunned, amazed. I went into the parlor, fearful, and looked – it was deserted. My bronze clock on the table read precisely three o'clock.

Had it been a warning? Was it still there, asking for my company so as not to go alone through those streets under the inclement sadness of a winter sky—she who had come for the sun, demanding the beautiful and vital light of our days?

Could it be? I called Alfredo and, nervous, as soon as I felt his footsteps in the hallway, I ran to the door to send him out with the message:

"Order a hearse by phone. Quickly! Is it near four?"

"Yes sir."

"Has Brandt come yet?"

"I think so, because the chalet is open."

"Then go. Order a coupé."

I refreshed my face and began to dress, worried about the sensation I had awakened.

In front of the mirror, without seeing myself, I thought: Oh, my nerves! My poor excited nerves were beginning to weaken in lukewarm cowardice. It was decidedly necessary to react. My soul, mastered by terror, weakened imbecilely before the most trivial incidents: the flight of an insect that knocked against the window made me shudder, at the click of a piece of furniture my blood ran cold. I gave the lapel of my frock coat a forceful pull and turned to the window.

The sun was breaking through the thinning clouds and the air was cool and soft. Great gaps of blue appeared and the glossy foliage glistened as tenderly as yesterday's shoots. Slow drips still fell at intervals.

I went down. In the living room, two Englishmen were absently smoking cigarettes and a boy, dressed as a sailor, leaned against the table and leafed through an issue of the *Graphic*.

I was on my way to the porch, to go to the cottage, when Brandt entered the room, still smoothing the rumpled sleeves of his tailcoat.

"Are we on time?"

"Yes."

Miss Barkley appeared, spoke to the Englishmen, who soon straightened up, and warned us:

"It is all ready. They are going to close the coffin. If you'd like to—"

"We'll accompany you."

On a narrow table, in the middle of the room, lay the black coffin, clad in foliage of silver. Women moved around, composing the flowers, stuffing them into the gaps, and the dead woman, very white, looked like wax. Her cheeks were sunken, with the bones protruding, and the eyes were sunken as well, half-open, as if unbuttoning in the lividity of the sockets. Her nose was very sharp, the lips thin, colorless, cracked and dry. A few strands of blond hair lit up her smooth forehead. Flowers were dying between her ebony hands, and a small golden cross rested on her shallow chest.

They closed the coffin. There were no tears. The Englishmen took it, lifting it up as a mere burden, Brandt and I backing them up. And off we went.

The women came to the porch. We passed among the lush rose bushes and the swaying branches dripped onto the coffin. One of the flowers dropped its petals, and just as the gardener opened the gate, in the arbor, a gladsome cicada gave its happy summer song, happy for the sun that came out in the blue, free as a boat that had opened wide sails into the wind and moved, airily, across the calm sea, away from the mist, away from the watery banks, away from the snowy cliffs, into the calm serenity of the smooth waters.

The neighborhood thronged to the windows, there were onlookers on the sidewalks. Miss Barkley waited for the last strap to be buckled, and when the coffin moved, she waved her hand as simple as if she were bidding farewell, for a few short hours, to one who was going into the dawnless night or the bright morning of a day that doesn't end.

When we returned to Rua do Marquês de Abrantes, we come

across the Public Health cart and a tray on a bench with disinfectants. I smiled, remembering Basilio's irritated words. Brandt muttered:

"The exorcism."

And, after a pause, he added in a mysterious tone: "If men could do the same to the heart, ridding it of longing, the soul would suffer less in its brief transit through the earth.

"Death is the Flower of The Tree of Life: it withers on the branch, leaves its petals in the grave, but the pollen reproduces it. The man who plows is not content, when he furrows and purges the field, to uproot the little plant: he digs at it, uproots the vine and the thinnest thread of root, and even sets fire to the stubble so that no harmful seed remains. The flower goes from here. Miserable flower! And off they go to destroy the lethal germs she left dispersed in the tiny room."

"Do you believe this, Brandt?"

"Yes, I believe! I believe, even if I judge Death to be an ascension, nothing more—what we call Life is the purification of being. Nature, that's all. The soul enters into existence as on a scale of perfection, it passes from the smallest to the greatest, oscillating between good and evil. In every man there remains a vague reminiscence of a previous life and there is a tendency towards the beyond: the earth holds us, the sky attracts us. The victory of the Absolute is Death.

"We were a tree, trying made us a bird, instead of captivating roots we acquired the loose wing, to win space. Man today, tomorrow..."

"Poetry..."

"Poetry is the flower of Truth, my friend, even if all ideas that stand out from vulgarity, the superior and the imbecile, are, through ignorance or derision, contemptibly attributed to it.

"The poet is a seer: he announces by symbols what is to be accomplished in the days to come. The flower has no earth, only aroma: the verse is pure abstraction—soul. The fruit, with the tasty pulp, comes later to the tree.

"Analyze any scientific law and you will find the poetic essence in it. The first sages were contemplatives: the word of Wisdom was born to the sound of lyres. Apollo guided the footsteps of infant Minerva. Everything is poetry."

The coupé slowed down among a throng of carts, held back by a wagon loaded with granite slabs that had caught one of its tall wheels. The wheel had sunk in a marsh that formed in front of the tangled scaffolding of a building under construction.

Live whips cracked along with furious shouts. There was, at last, a shriek of steel, a shout of cheers, and then the loud noise of many vehicles starting off in different directions. And the people fled to the sides haranguing. We followed.

Robustly, Brandt noted:

"It looks like we've left the city gates. Notice how everything here is different: another aspect, other types. The mud itself is black, as if made from coal dust."

The street, potholed and crooked, gleamed with a dark coating. We walked slowly past the large warehouses, between trucks that were rolling along with jerks and the screeching of irons.

Smeared coopers in leather aprons were hammering staves, scraping fifths, and an acidic, vine-like smell wafted from the vats.

Boatmen, in blouses or shirtsleeves, their robust tanned arms lined with turgid veins and their skin wrinkled in creases, piped or laughed at the procession in groups from the loading doors. In vast shady warehouses there were sacks tucked up against the roof in piles, between which were steep alleys.

In the sooty depths of foundries there were flaming pyres,

irons clanged through the rumbling noise of the machines.

Workmen trotted, hunched under the weight of sacks and, splashing in the mud, disappeared into old rambling buildings while other people, in a mighty coming and going, bumped into each other, in the docks or in the streets: bedraggled women, ragged children sniffing at the doors, gigantic blacks, with bare chests, dark and glistening with sweat, swayed with swollen biceps like piledrivers of strength.

Alleys, curved at a crossing, climbed sideways up the slope between a flat house with a slanted roof and the edge of a shack covered with grass. At the top, on the wild hillside, in dovecotes there were miserable homes—huts, cabins, lean-tos, crowded slums and a refuse of ruins in the dismantled disarray of a landslide.

Long chimneys, like obelisks, puffed thick coils of black smoke, and from moment to moment a hysterical scream shrieked over the noise, or the wailing of a siren sounded somberly.

When we arrived at the cemetery, we silently helped the two Englishmen remove the mud-splattered coffin, and, taking the handles, we climbed slowly up the rough, stony slope between a thick damp-washed wall and a flexing wall of bamboo.

The sun shone triumphantly, free from the clouds fleeing in defeat. The breeze blew softly.

Sad Cemetery of Exile!

Leaning against the mountain, it appeared accidental: sometimes crouched, in mounds, sometimes plunging into steep slopes, with abandoned and blackened tombs inside bushy mounds of wild grass, iron crosses gnawed by rust, the marble ones veined with blackness. It was as desolate as death itself in that dismal corner of the world, among twisted and shriveled trees, whose roots stood exposed, orphans of the earth washed away by the downpours.

The mountain, with a slender tower protruding from its

face, poured its barren flank into the cemetery. Ahead, the serene sea, through which a bridge loaded with wagons stretched far away, gleamed with boats. And further away, encompassing the smooth waters, were the laughing mountains, bluer than the sky.

We arrived at the naked chapel—lacking a symbol other than the sad iron cross at the apex of the pediment, stuck between the swallows that flew by.

Inside, were white walls with shutters, the place open at the top. There was only, in the center, a funeral table on which we rested the coffin.

The pastor, a pale man with a black beard and glasses, was waiting there, dressed in a white cloak with long sleeves, a black stole on his arm, the book between his fingers.

He reached the bier and began to read mechanically in a voice that faded, almost dying away, and then suddenly grew in a harsh, imperative tone, as if he were summoning the divinity to receive the soul he consigned.

It wasn't a prayer, it was more like a transaction with the beyond, in which the merchant could feel himself bragging about his merchandise, praising it, finally yielding it, with the annoyed sneers of those who give up the item for less than they want. He closed the book, and was soon gone.

We followed him with the light wagon, taking her up the slope to the ravine, next to the wall, where the open grave waited, with soft, muddy earth at the bottom, guarded by the gravediggers.

Again the pastor opened the book, muttered the extreme prayer, and slowly, in a silence in which the languid creak of the branches could be heard, we lowered the coffin, which floundered limply in the sodden grave.

The shovel of earth, passing from hand to hand, made the top of the bier resound five times. We walked away. Soon, in a hurry to finish, the gravediggers took up their hoes and a dull roar rang out.

The two Englishmen climbed the trail and, at the top, one of them, indifferent to the tombs, stretched out his arm, showing the landscape, explaining it to his companion and following with a stiff finger the twists of the earth, the smoke rolling from the chimneys, the black roofs, the gliding boats, the distant mountain range, the clouds themselves. The other stared.

On the branches, gilded by the sun, the cicadas sang ecstatically.

Brandt, standing before the naked and desolate chapel, which looked as if the desecration of a suicide had passed through it, shook his head:

"No! I do not understand religion without ritual, nor ritual without pomp. Man needs to *see* in order to understand and love. It is not enough to think of God, it is necessary to feel him, to have him before the eyes in material expression, as a target to which the prayer goes, to which the begging hands are thrown and the unleashed tears run in torrents."

"And Nature? All of this? The heavens and the earth?"

"All this is creation, not God. And this chapel is a deserted house, a dead body that is missing..."

"An idol..."

"The soul, old man, the soul of religions, which is precisely Poetry: an expression of Goodness, Love, Hope, Faith... the symbol, the symbol, the eternal and necessary symbol."

"This is desolately sad, I will agree. Let's go!"

And we descended disconsolately down the precipitous slope set in boulders.

In front of the car, Brandt hesitated for a moment; at last he said to the coachman:

"To the Globe!"

And, slumping into the seat, exhausted, he vented

"I'm hungry! I had a tremendous day! Fortunately, there is the sun. You can't imagine how bad I feel these days without light."

And, stooping to look at the sky, he exclaimed, enraptured by the blue: "A splendid afternoon!"

#

Scent and sound, living in the air, insinuate themselves more than light: the frond of a tree is a barrier to the sun—scent and sound pass through the strong walls of prisons.

In the brain, they are assiduous, and, visiting all the intricacies, they suggest ideas, awakening reminiscences, generating ecstasies and terrors, exciting jouissance or provoking tears.

There are melodies and aromas that renew nostalgia, others make us daydream, winging us into full fantasy.

A flowering garden inspires as much as an orchestra. And there are harsh sounds as there are aesthetic smells. The scent of the violet is a babble, the flowering jasmine is a bacchanalian chorus.

The thyrsus of the Maenads, made of sandalwood, was said to be encrusted with gardenias and carnations.

When I walked from the pure night air into the warm atmosphere of the house, I was immediately enveloped in the acrid smell of fumigation and chemical acids. Stunned, dizzy, I moved through the silent shadow of the room, with the gas on fire as at a wake, and crossed the corridor. I climbed the stairs to my rooms with the impression of walking along the funerary gallery of a tomb.

It was the heralding smell of Death that permeated the whole house.

My sitting room, despite the open window, stank. It was the mysterious "odor" fighting with the remnants of Death. A tremendous war of toxics against infinitesimals. Each atom was a battlefield.

Everywhere, the fight raged.

Undressing, with all the gas lit, around me I felt the fierce struggle. I imagined the exhalation of the corpse developing, taking over the whole house, invading it corner by corner, poisoning the air, the water, the light, all the essences of Life. But, at the same time, the astringent scent, which seemed to spur my sense of smell, reassured my extravagant thought that if lethal principles, penetrating my breath, brought ruin to my depths, in their dust armed opponents rushed and in the irritating smell that prickled my pituitary I felt their invisible spears, their swords, vibrating thrusts and blows, wounding from edge and point, without leaving a single one alive, not one! That would be enough to devastate my frail body.

I lay down. In the darkness, however, the fight raged even more, and in the hallucinatory state in which I remained, the sinister fantasy of my fearful delirium grew worse.

Before my eyes, in regiments blacker than the darkness, phalanxes passed by trampling, and a noise, as of anxious breathing, was the rumble of the retracted struggle.

Itching boiled in my body—they were the enemies. At times my chest would smother me as if an iron lid were weighing on it—it was the passage of fierce hordes.

My eyes burned, my ears rang.

Horrible, formidable battle! And so it must have been throughout the house, in the surroundings and in the deepest slats, and at all the points where the invisible ones treacherously groped, waiting for the opportune moment to attack, there was the smell, like the intensive breath of Life, puncturing, ravaging Death.

I fell into a deep sleep, thrashing about in the horror of an agonizing nightmare. The dead woman appeared to me immense and livid, as if illuminated by a halo of will-o'-the-wisp, naked, standing on a rough and arid cliff, scraping her body with her fingernails, throwing slabs of flesh, spatters of blood, locks of hair, teeth, fingernails. And wherever one of those patches fell, then, instantly, life ceased.

Men, by the thousands, bowed down, felled in tragic silence like weeds grown in a depleted field. Trees withered; clear waters of lively streams blackened into swamp; birds plucked their own wings and plunged from the air, dead.

At last, from the spear of the specter, the sky itself was bloodied with curds and soon the glowing stars were extinguished.

Then the torn-up skeleton began to move frantically, bobbing, gloating. She threw herself from the cliff onto the shroud and, stepping on it in triumph, danced and grew immeasurably, filling all the space until there was nothing left but the boneyard, overwhelming heaven and earth and, up there, where the ribs were like immense arches, was the huge, tabby skull, with two opaque eyes rolling in their sockets, like dead stars—corpses of the sun and moon, swaying and still illuminating in the last spasms.

I awoke in agony, drenched in a sweat of suffering and, throwing myself out of bed, I stood in the middle of the room, terrified and appalled, and still the hideous smell wafted astringently, making the air thick and prickly.

The shadows of night were already melting, dissolving into the laughing colors of dawn. I went out into the sitting room and, receiving the healthy breath of morning full in my face, I breathed in long gulps, greedily, as if I had surfaced after a long, suffocating dive.

I leaned out the window enjoying the wonderful apotheosis of dawn.

The sky, with the various shades of dawn, from soft purple to the gold brocade, lit up resplendent nature as if an immense screen of fire was slowly rising, overlapping the soft, faint blue.

The trees swayed in languid waves, their branches ruffled, and seemed to compose themselves brightly to receive the sun. The leaves, in the soft light that spread out in a swirl of gold, spread themselves with greedy eagerness.

From among the leafy branches, all the gliding birds of France suddenly broke, and they were chirping merry trills and their flights crossed each other in an air show, as the sky, clearer, was warmed by the Sun that rose in triumph.

I went down to the bathroom and, to dispel the funereal impressions, I decided to work all day, opening wide the doors of the "dream" that I had there, by hand, and taking refuge in it as among the flowering trees of a jungle of enchantment.

And I sat down at James' manuscript as the first ray of sunlight slashed through the open window.

CHAPTER VI

'Poets do not lie when they say that supernatural beings eagerly aspire to the contingent life of the ephemeral.

'The undine, in afternoon shadows, appears above the water and drifts into the floating weeds waiting for the swimmer. If she sees him, whether an airy nobleman or a rude, ragged defender, she gets excited, she looks at him with the pulse of desire in her turgid neck, her green eyes light up, her white cheeks turn pink and, when she sees him close by, leaping lightly over the stepping stones, passing quickly among the dense branches, she breaks her slender form from the grass. Standing, arching her bust in an imposing attitude, pushing back her dripping hair, she shows herself to him completely naked, invites him with a languid voice, seduces him with a lascivious gesture and, if she takes him in her arms, desperately embraces him, voluptuously girds him to her flesh and, pressing her cold lips to his mouth, sucks his life in kisses.

'Is it because she lacks lovers in her limpid retreat that she knows how to find them on earth? Let the village girls respond who, after the welcoming call, do not risk going to the river's edge so that the undine that crouches in the grass on the damp banks does not betray them.

'The fairies, to whose prestige all nature obeys, hide with annoyance the love of geniuses. One sees them in the very cold moonlight, wandering volatile in the mist, dancing around the lakes, singing and playing subtle instruments.

'They desire the ardent loves of the earth and attract mortal beings with incantations, seeking in them what they cannot find in sylphs and elves, the voluptuousness that enervates, the voluptuous sister of Death, more violent than the cold and barren love of the immortals.

'Always the opposite is preferred—desire is a loose, capricious bird that flies to contrast.

'How many times, looking from the top of the splendid tower where all joys surrounded me, I envied the sad fate of the little shepherd who passed through the valley, dressed in his worn coat, treading the snow on the rough path that led to the farm or the miserable cliff, untidy and without fire?

'Accustomed to prodigy, I was no longer surprised by the most extraordinary events of my captive life.

'To see, as I saw, in the fading of a twilight, the immense shadow of a bird whose plumes radiated; to see it launch at the thunderhead, ignite it with its stern on fire, scrape the glass windows with its golden claws and then shake noisily, leaving a trail of fire in space, was, for me, a spectacle as ordinary as the gushing of gargoyles on rainy days. I was distracted, and I took in the slow flight of wild ducks, which came up from the lakes in flocks and disappeared behind the hills, standing out for a moment in black dots against the glowing background of the sunset.

'Were these wonders for those who lived in them, if my days and nights were always a continuous wonder?

'Thus, the first impression I had when passing from the chamber to the salon where, windows, wide open, breathing pure and fresh air, I received the cheerful sun and the perfume of the flowered meadows and was given to my eyes the delight of contemplation of the blue sky over which was superimposed, in relief, the outline of the hills, was that it was just for fun. But soon, remembering the eve of a wild winter, a night of wind and snow, and remembering the dismal apparition that had walked with me, I shuddered.

'How had the thick snow melted in hours? How had the wild wind soothed into a gentle breeze? How had the sprawling groves of trees that were falling to earth, recovered now, all leafy and in bloom? How, from the barren winter, did heaven and earth pass, in the course of sleep, to the beauty and freshness of spring?

'I was looking, enthralled, when I heard footsteps and soon

I smelled Maya's adored scent. I turned around. It was her. She was smiling, beautiful with a rose in her lap and, gracefully placed at her belt a bunch of yellow carnations. I asked her about the transition that had taken place so quickly and she said calmly:

'"If there was a miracle, it was your three-month sleep. You fell asleep when the crows were still scratching the snow. The first swallows came and found you sleeping. The voice of the lark did not rouse you, nor did the nightingale, trilling in the rafters, manage to lift you out of the lethargy into which you had fallen. Fields and hills were green, trees and hedges were covered with flowers, the streams that you had left behind flowed swiftly, with festive haste. Swarms of bees invaded your rooms, butterflies swarmed around your bed and... you slept. Three long months you slept."

'"And why did my sleep last so long?"

'"Because you have discovered the face of Death."

'These words, uttered in a mysterious tone, left me stunned, and the whole scene of my last night came to my memory, without omission of detail—the fearful pilgrimage through the glowing halls, the funereal and dreadful spectacle of the coffin, the corpse of Arhat, the apparition at the entrance of my chambers.

'Shivering, feeling a sharp pain, cold as iron, that pierced my chest, stiff, almost voiceless, I asked about the strange man.

'"You must wait," said the maiden, looking at me sadly, her eyes clouding over. "Come with me and bid farewell to everything around you, and to me as well, who loves you, because you will never see again all that you are going to leave. The cocoon will open to free the butterfly. You will know what you desire. Come!"

'And, without another word, she advanced quickly, through the door, along the gallery, down the long, twisting stairs, and I followed.

'Below, in the courtyard of the idols, she stopped, extended *her cold hand to me, and her beautiful eyes—which still light up my soul as the dead stars shine at the bottom of the sky—seemed to dissolve in tears.*

'A moment our joined hands were clasped. We looked at each other in silence, but a figure appeared among the ivy that covered the arch of the stone and bronze gatehouse, and in it I recognized Arhat, in whose hand a long-stemmed lily of incomparable whiteness was held.

'I shuddered. At an imperative nod from the dominating man, I left Maya's cold, trembling hands and followed submissively toward prestige.

'Side by side we walked.

'The park gleamed in full sunlight, revived in all its myriad splendors. The scents rose with a soft exhalation, permeating the air.

'Vainly, narcissistic, with their variegated tails spread out in a flaming flabellum, peacocks lay motionless on the edge of the lake where airy white swans, pacing the waters slowly, glided serenely as if carried by the breeze.

'Pheasants flew from branch to branch with a flash of iridescent feathers; and from here and there and elsewhere, crossing in their flight, were birds with multicolored plumage, butterflies, bees, all winged beings enjoying the light, under the vivid dust of the sun, as in ardent baptism of fecundity.

'Arhat walked abstractedly, his gaze rapturous. From time to time, from the lily he took long, greedy sniffs.

'Even though we were following a sandy path, under which my footfalls rattled, the Master's walk was silent and, for a moment, as we stood shoulder to shoulder, I didn't feel his body but instead a soft, pleasant heat like a ray of sunlight falling on me. A single shadow bordered me, blackening the earth. On Arhat's side, preceding him, there shone a light, and around him

the leaves gleamed with a mysterious glow.

'We walked slowly through a secluded lane laid with gleaming gravel and came to a clearing where the fine grass spread on carpet so velvety that walking through it was pure delight.

'Not infrequently, among the branches, two large eyes, moist and gentle, peered at us—some antelope or doe.

'The branches creaked softly in the breeze, and an acrid, wild smell stung the atmosphere like the fragrant breath of healthy trees.

'There were no other souls, only the animals enjoyed the beauty of that blazing morning in the lushness of the park, whose aspects varied as we advanced, leaving to one side or another shadowy depths of woods or vast plains of flats, mirrored lakes or waves of foaming waters curling on grass-bristled rocks, a thatch or a grotto, yawning or gentle. We went rolling over hills of such soft grass, under the hue of the flowers, that at the first glance, one immediately sensed the work, the capricious care of man.

'Flocks of little deer took their revenge on the hedges, crossed the paths into thorns, running over each other and sending fluttering wings in a skittish shake, the roars of alarmed birds, flights of insects, rustling of lizards and, far away, in the shade of a branching oak, deer rested, chewing their cud. One in front, with a firm and lofty head, looked hostile, as if spying on our steps and ready to invest in defense of the tribe of which he seemed the mighty chief.

'But Arhat continued on, and I, not in the mood to speak, followed his path, worried if not fearful, imagining absurdities.

'We approached a fountain, which whispered hidden among the sweet plants that were damp from the continuous roar. He stopped with his eyes on the ground, quiet, his head bent in thought.

'After a moment he turned to face me, beckoned me to sit on a rock, seating himself on another, and after sniffing the lily, said:

'"One afternoon—I was then residing in a suburb of London and it was early winter, night came down early—I was studying alone when I heard a rumbling in the street, horrified exclamations, terrified screams. I rushed to the window and, opening it, saw in the black mud, to which gulfs of blood were added, two dying bodies. A big car disappeared in a rush, pursued by the public clamor and, as it was the hour to leave the factories and workshops, in a short time a dense crowd formed at the site of the accident.

'"I had, in my company, a Tibetan colossus who served me with dedication and worship. I called him and, showing him the corpses, ordered him to bring them to me. I don't know how it happened, but he didn't spend more time coming and going than necessary.

'"I took the remains to my study and, examining the bodies attentively, I recognized that one was a boy, whose head had been left in a smashed state. The other, a girl, had her chest crushed: it was a mass of flesh bristling with splinters of bones, bleeding in gushes.

'"Making use of the notions I have from Magna Science, that is Alchemy, and as I still found traces or rather manifestations of the presence of the seven principles, I retained the force of jiva, or vital principle, causing it to attract the others who then circulated, in an aura, around the flesh and, with the urgency that inspired, I took use of the parts of the bodies that had not been touched. Taking the girl's head and adapting it to the boy's body, I reestablished the circulation, revived the fluids and thus, retaining the principles, from the Athma, which is the divine essence itself, I rebuilt a life, in a man's body, which is now you."

'Such a strange revelation, made in such a serene tone, with the simplicity of a natural conversation, shook me in such a way that I felt as if I was drained and in darkness, but a subtle aroma, *penetrating me sweetly, restored my breath. I opened my eyes again: Arhat was at my side, bending over my face the lily whose perfume delighted me.*

"'Listen," he continued. "I will not tell you the mystery, it is written. Here, you have it." He bent down and, pushing aside the foliage that overgrew the fountain, displayed a silver-laminated cedar box, opened it and took out a book which he handed to me.

"'I wanted to give you the knowledge of what is exposed in this volume, which is your Bible, you observed my transit with curiosity and I had to return, in the 'aura' of the Beyond, to help my body, which was still mine and which you profaned with a reckless look.

"'Your punishment was kind: three months in Death's prisons, but what you lost is priceless. You benefited me, by lightening the hours of the great and definitive Renunciation.

"'Before the sun touches the pinnacle of the sky, I will have freed myself from this step of anguish by integrating myself with Athma. The body being earth, what is life more than a prison in a tomb? You have shortened the time of my ascension.

"'Life is a sequence of activity and inertia, a necklace in which black and luminous beads, day and night, are interspersed. Each night that passes brings you into a new morning. Reincarnations are great states in which we purify ourselves, we pass from one to the other through the shadow of death, which is the night, at the end of which the dawn shines. The day without end, light shining, clear and serene and infinite day, will only dawn after the cycle of material existences has been completed— when purity, by expiation, becomes equal to that of initiation— when the candor of old age equals the candor of the cradle.

"'From sleep you pass into the morning with memory, which is the awareness of the past. Death, which is a longer sleep, erases this vestige of life, so that, in reincarnations, there are vague reminiscences which cannot be certain: stigmas persist, but

the memory fades."

'He took a long breath of the lily and continued: "My exile is close, I must therefore be brief and as clear as the word will allow me. You have your whole life in this book, but the ideogram in which it was written can only be deciphered by someone who has reached perfection.

"'If you manage to discover a privileged intelligence that interprets symbols, you will be in the world like an angel among men, lord of all graces, of all prestige, a sovereign will in a wonderful spirit; but if you do not obtain the key to the arcane, woe is you!'"

'He fixed his sharp eyes on my face, and for a long time he looked at me. Motionless, only the lily swayed in his hand in a pendulum rhythm.

'After a moment, he continued: "On the same night that I managed to make the conjunction of the two bodies, which belonged to Death, and which I reintegrated into Life, yielding to the earth the tribute that was due to it as the pieces were buried by my faithful servant, I left my home, coming to inhabit this ancient castle where, at the cost of my own essence, at the expense of my energy, I have been feeding you the life you have today, giving you my essence with the same loving disinterest with which the maternal bird digs its claws in its chest and pecks at the wound, causing the blood to burst with which it feeds the nest.

"'You are truly the son of my soul.

"'As soon as you established yourself in life, however, an incorrigible doubt assailed me about the soul that should influence your existence, giving it its moral character.

"'Two souls wandered around the wreckage of the flesh, obeying the prestige of Karma, which is the force of integration. But one alone could prevail, since of the two independent lives only one could subsist. Since the signs of the action of the seven *principles that act on matter appeared in the remade body, the existence of a soul was evidently proved. Which one would be victorious—the man's or the woman's?*

"'All my attempts to discover this mystery have failed. I watched long nights, I lost long and consecutive days bent over your cradle, casting for possibilities in vain. My senses were heightened, but what could I obtain from an infant's psychic inertia?

"'Dorka, who attentively accompanied you from the first hours with the solicitude a priestess gives to the voice of the oracle, died uncertain, without obtaining even a clue that would give rise to the slightest suspicion.

"'I endeavored to place the two sexes at your side, looking for the most perfect examples of beauty and grace, flexibility and poise, gentleness and decorum, the fragile candor that surrenders and the haughty strength that dominates: Siva and Maya. Seeing them, I convinced myself that the soul that assists you, whatever it was, would betray its nature by inclining to contact one or the other.

"'It wavered in ephemeral affection, in whims of aesthesia rather than love. You never showed a predilection and the flesh remained impassive in the presence of either one or the other, even if the gaze sometimes exalted itself just admiring, ecstatic in the beauty, showing the same rapture with which it soaked in the landscape or the vivid colors of the sky at dawn and in the afternoon.

"'In your face, the feminine beauty was accentuated more and more, but the body was strengthened in masculine vigor and the heart was always silent, inert, indifferent, the golden thread between the two sexes that were paired up, disputing each other.

"'Perhaps only now are you being defined. You have entered puberty, which is the time when the soul unbuttons, revealing itself to be loving, lighting the fires of voluptuousness in

the flesh.

"'If the feminine predominates in you, which shines through in the beauty of your face, the face of your sister, you will be monstrous. If you conquer the spirit of man, as the vigor of your muscles would have you believe, you will be like a magnet of lust. But unhappy you will be, as there has been no other in the world, if the two souls that hovered over the revived flesh managed to both insinuate themselves into it.

"'The Linga-sharira, *the astral body or ambient 'aura', which circles in a halo around the head, is the last principle that leaves the body—and your head is feminine. But is your heart a manly heart?*

"'Woe to you if the two principles manage to penetrate you—discord will walk with you as the shadow follows the body. Loving, you will be jealous and disgusted with yourself. You will be an incoherent anomaly: wanting with your heart and hating with your head, and vice versa. Your right hand will declare war on the sinister one, one of your cheeks will be on fire with shame and disgust, while the other will be inflamed with the modesty that is the flowering of desire. You will live between two bitter enemies.

"'There! That is you... Tell me, where does your heart take you? What do your senses claim? Where do your misty dreamlike eyes linger more charmingly?"*

'He stared at me questioningly, and when he got no word from my terrified silence, he shuddered, and there was a cerulean flash.

"'It's late!" he sighed at last, and said wistfully, "The lily begins to fade and droops. The life in it goes away!*

"'I lacked a body to support me like a bird needs a branch to land on, I chose the flower and now the flower withers."*

'Indeed, the lily bowed languidly, and bent on the stem, limp, turning yellow. Arhat, as if to take advantage of its last moments, intoned these words, pronouncing them poignantly:

"'Goodbye! I prevented everything so that you would not suffer. There is suffering enough in what you have before you. You will find someone to guide you through your first steps out of your paradise. The fortune I bequeath to you guarantees you the joys of life and the servility of men. You will see them bend before you like a field of wheat in the wind, and you will pass by, trampling prejudices and conventions, honor, love, justice and laws, strength and pride, innocence and misery and, far from crying out against disgrace, the nobles, the honest, the pure, the insulted spouses, the infamous virgins, the judges, the patriots converted to infamy by your extortion will bless the affront, and what's more they will proclaim your virtue the more you harass them in the golden swamp.

"'That vile gold! Do to it what the sun does to a flame: light, clarity, heat, life. The gold in the mine is the real fire of this cursed region. Be its sun, with your celestial light, applying yourself to the good. Be good.

"'A coin is the wheel that leads to all infamy and salvation: placed on the edge of the abyss, it rushes over, thrown into the sky it becomes is a star. Be good. Go and search the vast land for the one who will give you the key to the secret that closes the mystical book. Now follow me. I want to leave you where you should be so that your guide can find you."

'He went forward, taking the lead, and I saw that, as he went away, the light that illuminated the forest and drove off the shadows and the cold of winter afternoons, went with him.

'It wasn't his body that impeded the view of the landscape, showing itself to me through him as if through a gilded glass window. The branches lit up by the light of his chest, his feet were two splendors that made the gravel shine, his hands refracted iridescent rays, brightening the bushes over which they hovered.

'Diaphanous and luminous, when near me he produced

only a mild sensation of heat. Sometimes he got confused with me, or I stepped through him, and I felt as if I were in full sun and my shadow disappeared into the earth.

'The lily wilted. Arhat, taciturn, seemed to float on air—his feet together, motionless, not even touching the ground, straight, inflexible and his head erect and blazing, he walked beside me like an ethereal being, freeing himself from what was human in him, acquired in Humanity, jettisoning from the staring eyes, through the splendid face, thick tears that rolled, glistened in diamonds, fell on the sand or grass and kept shining.

'We arrived at a clearing. He made a flashing gesture with his straight arm, indicating a rough path, along which I followed, bowing as if to a threat.

'A few steps away I shivered, hearing a long, torn sigh. A strange force held me back: I turned and, amazed, terrified, I saw the luminous figure of the Master rising in slow ascent and fading, little by little fading—only translucent flickering, like the exhalation of the scorched earth in the late hours, it hovered, but by volatilizing, it became subtle and completely disappeared. The lily alone was suspended in the air, swaying slightly. Suddenly, like a wounded bird, it swooped down and, touching the ground, breaking apart.

'Instantly the trills and nightingales of birds vibrated in concert, the deer roared fiercely among the gloomy oaks, and the air became most fragrant.

'As for me, it was as if I had been blinded, gagged, restrained. I plunged into abrupt darkness, breathless, paralyzed, feeling myself stunned by a somber hum as if a shell had been fitted to my ears or I lay a prisoner in the echoing and tenebrous galleries of a catacomb. What happened? I don't know.

'When I woke up, I was crossing, at a broad trot, a smooth and white road, between flowering hedges and cottages sheltered in the shade of trees.

'The soft afternoon was all aroma; and in the still air, at intervals, a bell sang. Swallows fluttered and under the blue mist the fields slept.

'In front of me, motionless and grave, a fair-haired man with thin whiskers held on his knees a box in which I immediately recognized the covers of the book of my destiny.

'The words of the Arhat immediately returned to me, as if attentive in memory awaiting my appeal: "I want to leave you where you should be, so that your guide may find you."

'This was the man who should safely introduce me into the world that already seemed complicated and hostile to me.

'As if in answer to my questioning gaze, he tilted his head slightly and muttered, "Sullivan." It was his name. Then, as if to relieve himself of an uncomfortable weight, he took out of his pocket a padded black leather wallet and handed it to me, explaining: "From the Bank of England. Millions, the Arhat's fortune."

'And as far as London, where we arrived with the night, we didn't exchange a word.

'We stopped at the Ambassador Hotel, where they were already waiting for us with the largest, sumptuously tailored rooms. And real life began for me.

'Comparing it, during my concentrated and longing silences, with the one I left behind forever, it seemed to me more extraordinary and prodigious.

'My days in the lost manor passed into dormancy with the monotony with which the waters of a clear, beautiful, but always, invariably serene, river flow, and with the same tearful murmur, with the same candid flowers carried along the course, the same green branches supporting them. On the smooth surface and in the whirlwind into which I had thrown myself, surprises followed one another, minute after minute.

'The first four days of my new existence were, it should be said, fuller than the quiet eighteen years spent in the dreary manor of the sad valley.

'Sullivan showed me everything: the most imposing splendor and the most touching and sordid misery.

'I saw processions of princes and waves of galleys, one and the other brandishing weapons. I heard choirs in cathedrals vast as cities, and I heard the panting of boats crossing the river, the sad chant of workers around the workshops. I heard the tinkle of gold and iron. I roamed the city and its bowels—sometimes on the surface of the earth with the sky overhead, sometimes underground with a tomb vault weighing down on my chest. And I saw, with true astonishment and revolted pity, the machine conquering man, the machine making misery, grinding the poor to enrich the rich. The machine that relegates effort, as gunpowder has rendered bravery useless.

'Water, fire, the ethereal spark, all pure forces combined for crime, stealing bread from the poor, stealing his clothes, taking his home, throwing him on the road as naked and as destitute as if he were bitter from birth.

'I visited factories and workshops, and I was moved by the inhuman devices that, like the plow, turning over and furrowing the earth, kills the humble herbs so that the bread harvest grows without parasites, dislodging the weak for the benefit of the strong. I saw everything.

'We left the opulent squares and wallowed in the disgusting alleys where dwelt a dismal, spectral, painful people. Vermin: men, women, children holding filthy rags to their emaciated nudity, stretching out their starved hands, surrounding us, croaking requests, charging with sinister faces or crawling, crying.

'Hideous beings spilled out of the lumbering huts, some scrawny, shivering with fever, others an apoplectic purple, staggering drunk, hoarsely clumsy or spouting curses. Impoverished, ragged little girls who took us by the arm with wanton cynicism—children who had not known innocence—squeezing their skeletal breasts, lustfully winking their languid eyes, shamelessly nibbling their livid lips.

'We fled, harassed by the ragged and soon we emerged in the splendor of the city.

'A bitter taste remained in my soul from such visions. And I only truly understood the world as "supernatural."

'The "natural" must have been the happy life I had lived with the Master, served by all the wonderful forces of heaven and earth, granted all my desires, comforted in my sorrows, sheltered from the cold, protected from the sun, strong and healthy and, around me in the most bitter winter, the flowers blooming and the fruits ripening. Listening with delight to the sweet song of the birds. The natural person remained there with the enchantments, with the prodigies highlighted by Goodness.

'Only then did the supernatural appear to me in the shadow of the temples of God, at the crushing feet of inflexible Justice: it was that—a scale with two opposing shells: in one, weighing, to lift the other to happiness, misery, tears, only tears. The supernatural was that.

'In the vast hall of the hotel, in the dazzling glow of the lights which were reproduced on the trains and flashed on the marble, between the flowered tables where the tableware gleamed and the crystals sparkled, the affluence was incessant: men, in formal attire, with large roses in their buttonhole, women in dresses that stripped their necks and backs open. A hidden orchestra played smoothly.

'Sullivan, always impassive, was indifferent to the mess that stunned and unnerved me.

'Outside, at night, the party grew with a continuous,

screeching noise. All the time, in the happy chatter, bottles were detonated amid chuckled laughter.

'It was the bountiful hour of the gift—the gold melted in joy. And in the square, cars passed between aisles of beggars, running with purity to vice or watching for the opportune moment of theft or violent robbery, at gunpoint, in the shadows.

'Sullivan, as soon as we had finished the melancholy dinner, invited me to the "night's entertainment." We went to theaters, concert halls, colossal circuses, erotic cafes. I followed, dragged along. At first everything dazzled me, but the admiration dissolved into boredom like the dust that a wind lifts from the road and, for a moment, ripples, shines golden in the sun, and then falls to the ground.

'Silence attracted me. Shy, irritated, vexation made me retreat, fleeing from the outrageous eyes of the onlookers, noticing demeaning shamelessness in the malicious insistence with which men stared at me, lewd impudence in the ecstasy of women who stared at my face with scandal.

'I saw the nocturnal orgy, the stage of vice in all its forms: in the loose debauchery in which women and young men huddled together, in the naked drunkenness, in the unbridled copulation and its result, and then, through the silent darkness, in splashing steps, stumbling figures sniffing, turning over rubble, disputing with dogs over the shit in their cups.

'Returning to the hotel with a heart full of sadness, I couldn't get to sleep and leaned over the balcony contemplating the vast city, splendid with lights, whose misery I had uncovered in all its hideousness and I kept thinking about the horror of an ulcerated body, glistening under the rays of light like a rot that resolved itself into sparks, an immense carrion exhaling the luminous miasma of the will-o'-the-wisp.

'The supernatural!

'Worries faded whenever my eyes found the strange book. Then, remembering the words of the Arhat, I focused my attention on the symbols, seeking to reveal their secret, questioning them with desperate eagerness.

'How many times have I fallen asleep in their impenetrable pages!

'One day I decided to consult the most vaunted sages who claimed to be experts in Veiled Science and, for months, I walked through palaces and mansards with the sealed book, listening to notables and modest investigators, and they all returned me to the horror in which I lived, aggravating it even more with their words, which had given me hope.

'Sullivan, in spite of his grave manner and severe appearance of austerity, took only joy in worldly pleasures, and every morning, even though I had no dealings in the city, he brought me a voluminous correspondence. And I, opening my letters at random, read invitations to parties, complaints of miseries, lewd proposals, requests from handlers of gold, and my hands came out of that paperwork wet with their tears and stained with their mud.

'Sullivan didn't say a word, but smiled at the seductions that besieged me. I felt the encouragement with which he pushed me to the disgusting filth.

'One day, disgusted with the material man who clung to life, and burning more intensely with the urge to know my destiny, I decided to go out into the world, go on a long pilgrimage, go through all the seats of Ancient Science where, perhaps, I would find the knowledge predestined to hand over the arcane key.

'I sent my guide away with a check on the Bank of England, which assured him the abundance of means to focus on his enjoyment, and embarked, philosophically, to the Orient. Two years, without a day's rest, I walked through rough hills and tangled thickets, I wandered, from sea to sea, the great continent *of Asia, visiting the recesses of the contemplatives, consulting sages and penitents, leaving the forest to enter the shrines. I delved into ancient wild Thessaly. I walked through the log huts of the snow countries. I slept in the warm oases of sandy Africa. I heard sibyls and seers. I talked with the mystics of the frozen North where, at the mercy of the icebergs, by the coldness of the white nights, diaphanous spirits fly and I found in man only the superficial knowledge of life. And my soul? Ah, me!*

'It was in Stockholm that I felt my misfortune when I fell in love for the first time and that love... that love could only be generated in a female soul.

'So... my sister is the victor in me.

'Affectionately welcomed in the intimacy of a noble family, whose coat of arms dates back centuries, I found in the young representatives of this august house the best friends that I have come across.

'They were twins and beautiful! Love entered me as into the virginal heart of the maiden, but it was to the young man that my soul was devoted, the young man who had made me the confidant of his affection for others.

'My soul struggled in greedy anxiety if he did not appear, and I exalted myself in violent fury hating him, hating him and execrating myself with disgust, as if I felt polluted.

'His confidences stung me bitterly and every word of tenderness with which he alluded to his affection hurt me like a dart stuck in my heart and the name of his bride alone was a torture that was excruciating to me.

'Poor me! Oh, my strong soul, my virile soul, where are you if you don't defend me?

'I ran away from the sweet brothers, I ran away from sweetness, from candid love, ashamed as a clumsy man and unhappy with that forbidden love. And, shutting myself up, I

agonized over the volume, staring at the symbols to extract from them the Truth, whatever it was, the solution to the terrible problem of my soul or of the twin souls that fight in the revolting arena that is my miserable heart.

'*I fled. Since then my life has become unbearable. Suffering took care of the interpretation of the symbols: I know that I am a wretch, the one of whom the Arhat said: "You will be as unhappy as none other in the world."*

'*Each flower has its own perfume, a life cannot obey two rhythms. Two struggling souls, feeling differently, render useless the instinct which is the principle of attraction.*

'*A monster, a monster that devours itself, that's what I am.*

'*The book can't say any more—that's all, and that's the horror.*

'*Imagine a bird that, when it left its nest, felt its feet entangled in steel wires and, anxious, attracted by the blue, beat its wings until it died exhausted. So I will end up in the void, flying captive, neither in the sky nor of the earth, neither from the tree nor from the ether, trapped in space and in the branches...*'

CHAPTER VII

The afternoon was fading languidly, saturated with scent, melancholic with the dimming of colors when I retreated from the table, hunched and pushing back the laborious pen, my mouth bitter and scorched from smoke, my head dazed and thundering in a vacuum.

Spirit and body both chafed at the strenuous work. Softly, I leaned back against the chair, legs outstretched and head bowed, and I remained so in unfocused rest, reviewing the novel's dream in which I had been enraptured, converting the gleaming words of James' wonderful original into the pale and poor sayings of my petty version from the early hours of the morning until that violet and dreary twilight. Only a sober lunch, taken hastily in the room, had interrupted.

I still smoked a cigarette distractedly, listening to the trill of the swallows close by, my eyes ecstatically focused on the trembling brightness of a lonely little star that had shyly just appeared and which seemed vexed and afraid of being the only one in that immense desert of the sky, still warm from the sun and streaked with tinges of purple, like the bloody arena of a coliseum.

There were children in the neighborhood, and their sounds were as sweet and voluptuous as the slow rustle of palm trees in the wind.

Vague sounds drifted in hesitantly in the silence. Little by little they grew, sometimes confused, in noise and sometimes distinct in melody, clear in their airy vibrations, accentuating or fading as if they were oscillating in space. They erupted with a roar, openly thundered in clangor as sound blasts of brass and drums burst into a clatter, and then the sounds died away again, leaving in the mystical air of the afternoon, in the calm tranquility of that suburban street, a martial echo like a passing parade of a triumphant army on a tranquil plain of a peaceful village. The sound sheltered in the shade of trees, rocked, gently, by the muted *levadas*.

It was a military band that took the tram to Botafogo.

I stretched, yawning wildly, and rising to my feet, staggered with numb steps to the window, where I leaned in ecstatic contemplation.

The palm trees looked like bronze, still gleaming in the last glow of the sun. Pigeons passed each other in serene flight, and the scent that rose from the water-soaked earth was as fresh and pleasant as the breath of health.

The bell rang downstairs for dinner.

I felt sluggish, not in the mood to move, trapped in that serenity and enraptured with the curiosity of a new spectacle: the rising of the stars, the fading of the bright colors of the sun, the slow spreading of the shadow that blackened more and more and more and more.

Soon the humble voices awoke in the shallow grass—the nocturnal song of the little *luras*, the crickets, that play with silence and rhythm like the monotonous tick of a dark clock. And the fireflies lit up among the branches, carrying their stray flashes to all dark corners.

The gardener scraped his cutlass with a shuddering ring, singing softly.

Again the bell sounded.

I made slight ablutions, dressed myself in an annoyed slump, as if I had barely slept, and leaving the parlor, which reeked of smoke, I slowly descended the stairs, feeling the steps yield to my limp, rubbery stride.

Guests began to approach the already lit dining room, the dishes white on the smooth tablecloth among fresh flowers that colored and perfumed the modesty of the guest table.

Voices drew me to the porch where a group was arguing. The

subject was a telegram and Pericles, exalted in patriotism, his tie fluttering at loose ends, boomed hyperbole that recalled our epic history: hard-fought battles, deeds of bravery, boasts and acts of temerity. With wild gestures he marked the resistance, and the courage without arrogance, of the caboclo from the North and the brazen advance of the cavalrymen from the South, the *gauchada brava*, whose spear, in the indomitable throw of the charge, stops the most courageous from wounding them in the melee. Red and apoplectic, with turgid purple veins, he crumpled the newspaper in which he had read the telegram, threw it violently to the ground as if he had thrown, with disgust, a spiked gauntlet at the feet of the infamous ribald.

They all laughed at the gesture and he, even more incensed, bulged his watering eyes and began to punch his chest with a hollow sound, offering it to the spears and shrapnel of the scoundrels who dared to defy the Fatherland.

"If there's a war, I'll leave everything and enlist! My patriotism is not just words..."

"It's made of sheet metal," countered Basílio mockingly, his belly shaking with laughter.

Pericles gasped, glaring at the bookkeeper, whose fat, puffy face swelled ironically.

"Look, my friend, during the revolt I spent a lot of night on the Caju lines, gun in hand. I'm not one of those people who flee into the woods when they smell gunpowder. I don't write out my intentions, not me. If there is war... I march!"

"Come now, get over it," countered the Commander, sulking. And stretching up on tiptoe, with his chest curved, he inquired: "War with whom? Why?"

"With whom? You dare ask?"

"Yes, with whom?"

Pericles took a long step and, in a tragic attitude, pointed his finger at the newspaper, crumpled in a ball next to the balustrade:

"Read the telegram. It's there!"

"What telegram? That's just hoodwink. It's all trickery, politics, negotiations. The country may need it, but it is arms, strong arms that work the land, taking advantage of all this uncultivated wealth that exists. Quit your bravado, my friend."

"Bravado?!"—and he bit his livid lips. "If you were Brazilian..."

The Commander shot the contractor a tremendous look, his arms crossed, his fingers hooked as if in painful claws, and stepping forward he burst, in a rage, shouting hoarsely:

"No, I'm not Brazilian, but I love this country much more than the gentleman who wants to bloody it, raze it and"—in a fury, he roared—"hand it over to the English!"

The other recoiled, gaping.

"Yes, sir... to the English! I have here everything that is mine, my fortune and my life, everything, do you understand, Monsieur Pericles? All! And you?"

He leaned back in judgment, his eyes fixed on the builder's stupefied face. He passed his hand over his shiny bald head for a moment but kept his gaze fixed on the pale face of the patriot, who was breathing heavily and, bending at the chest, supercilious and hostile, his lips vibrated in a palpitation of rage, and you could feel the violence of a decisive insult building. But finally he said, "You know what, my friend?"—there was a momentary pause and the commander concluded: "Let's go partake of the soup, which is better, before it gets cold."

It was a relief for everyone and Basilio, to finish things with a joke, commanded: "To the ranch!" And everyone entered the dining room, laughing.

Fortunately for the contractor, who was repressing the humiliation of the Commander's onslaught, Brandt appeared with the always garrulous Decio who, while still at the door draped in a light flannel costume, asked Miss Barkley's permission to offer him a bunch of red carnations from Petrópolis, which he brought, in clusters, to the man's buttonhole.

At the noisy entrance of the student, a broad smile lit up all their faces. The Englishwoman herself, ever sullen, wrinkled up her emaciated face, revealing her teeth, large and yellow as beans, in the curl of her pale lip.

"I am asking Miss forgiveness for my ungrateful absence. The end of the year is approaching and it is necessary that I steal a few hours from all this sweet love and tender friendship to consecrate them to the sordid diseases, to the Human Pain that will be the guarantee of my smiling Future."

The student sat down, opened his napkin and glancing at the audience, while the servant served him the soup, murmured to himself amiably, saying: "All is good around here. This is the house of Hygia, the temple of beneficial health."

Basilio muttered:

"It's a barracks, doctor. We are threatened with going out into the field with weapons. Our friend Pericles is going to enlist in the army and we, out of solidarity, are going with him."

The Commander chuckled over the roast and the contractor, resuming his haughty bearing, passed the napkin over his lips and, after greedily chewing the morsel held in his mouth, exclaimed:

"It is true!"

"Enlist? But, Lord, why?"

"I may help!" he answered. And then, heatedly: "Myself and all true patriots." He straightened up, laying the cutlery on the table and, facing the student, asked: "Tell me, sir, as you are young, generous, and enthusiastic. In the event of war with a foreigner, will you go or stay?"

Decius sighed softly:

"I'd go."

"Dear God!?" Pericles responded firmly. "You won't stay!"

"I would not stay."

"Don't go! March! You'll be one of the first."

"According to the Gospel, my patriotism is not bellicose, my dear Mr. Pericles. I don't have the arms of Camões. Furthermore, the wars of this century, with the terrible engines that reinforce them, are tremendously deadly. Thus, it is necessary for a man to remain in his homeland as a seed to repopulate it and write, in the eternal pages, the superb epic of his elders. I will be that predestined man. As long as my patricians win—because I do not admit the possibility of defeat—I, in the desert silence of mother earth, will compose the perfect Alexandrians who will carry, through the centuries, the fame of heroes and their names. And on the day the troops return, I will go there to the Pharoux with a great lyre, naked and crowned with laurels, like Sophocles before the Greeks of Salamis. I will cross the Avenue, at the head of the armies, singing the paean of victory!"

Suddenly, rising up in repulsion, he said resentfully: "But you, who take the name of the great Greek who made Athens the capital of Beauty, have no right to think of wars, friend Pericles."

"Support!" snorted the Commander, getting stuck into his pudding.

"War is the reason of tyrants, the strength of barbarians. The intelligent man, the superior nations win with clear judgment and if they vibrate a sword it is that of the Law that only strikes evil, like a surgeon's scalpel. Let's not talk about wars. Let's talk about Love, about Beauty, the Beauty that is the charm of life."

"And if they insult us?"

"But no one insults us."

"Oh! No one insults us?"

"Nobody!" said the student, sternly.

"Haven't you been reading the papers?"

"No, my friend, I have not read, nor will I. My newspaper is the sky blue one. I read in it the days and nights, the beautiful articles of light and shadow that are the golden clouds and the bright stars. The rotating machine that interests me is the world. But on the subject of Beauty: How is our Breton Apollo? the handsome James, wonder of the city?"

"He went into Tijuca chasing butterflies," said the Commander.

"Hasn't he been home?"

"No."

"A strange man!"

Basilio smiled surreptitiously, lowering his head over his plate. Miss Barkley said:

"I think he may be leaving."

"Leave us?"

"Yes. To return to England."

"Why?"

"He's a freak."

The commander asserted:

"Crazy! Crazy is what he is, and swept away by madness."

"Why crazy, Commander?" asked Decio.

"Why? Does a man of sense do the things that he does? You ask why because you only know him by sight. Ask our friend who lives next door to him there."

Décio looked at me with questioning eyes and I replied:

"The Commander is wrong. Mister James is an excellent neighbor. I have no reason to complain."

"Well, I'm sorry I can't say the same, and I assure you that if he stayed in this house for another month, I'd be the one to move, since I don't have a hard head like a Turk. That devil of man doesn't sleep, he's kicking around the house all night. Go with God! Beautiful, yes... but unbearable!"

"Well, I," declared the student "would give years of my life to spend a day with him. He is a type that interests me, a strange being. His novel must be original." And then he emphasized. "Commander, beauty like that in a man... there is a divine mystery there! Happy is he who can penetrate it!"

Basilio, always sarcastic, cleaned himself with his napkin and maliciously ruminated on the student's sentence to the bristling ear of the commanding officer, who chuckled. But Brandt, who until then had remained aloof, eating slowly and eyes lowered, threw down his cutlery and, setting his chest at an ostensible height, faced the bookkeeper, whose smile slowly faded, as if basking in the folds of his fat cheeks.

They stared at each other, but the artist dominated his adversary, made him pale and lower his eyes, and across the table the scene was understood, although many did not understand the reason, not having noticed the perverse whisperings to the man, Commander Dicaz.

When we got up, Brandt, sullen, hands in his pockets, walked straight to the porch looking disgusted and, without waiting for coffee, went down to the garden, disappearing.

Décio, who had taken my arm, snatched me up to tell me about his current love, an incident that was required in all his conversations.

He exalted the divine woman, a frugal muse, inspiring his verses but always reminding him of death, binding him to her love with the avaricious and ineluctable greed with which the tomb takes possession of the corpse. She abandoned herself in his arms, with the passive lassitude of a victim aspiring to a martyrdom where the scandal of a surprise that would expose her to her husband's revenge, cast her, bloodied and naked, before the curious eyes of the world into the squalor of comment. A unique woman, romantic to the point of madness.

"Sometimes, gently pushing me away from her, she begins to cry in silence, more beautiful when adorned with tears. If I ask her why, she answers in a voice that moves and excites: 'I'm afraid!' And once she described to me her terror as reflected in a dream: 'We were caught. I saw him enter armed, I heard the sound of the revolver, I felt the pain of the wounds and the flowing heat of the blood, I agonized and died. After I was dead, however, I read the news in the newspapers describing all about our secret love, regretting that your talent was so soon stolen from the world, and my beautiful youth was so tragically damaged. And I saw both of us, side by side, cold, rigid, between candles of mercy on the slabs of the Morgue and, around us, the crowd crowing. And I still loved you, my heart, still and cold, I asked for yours while my parched mouth was thirsty for your kisses, my shrouded form demanded your body. It was horrible!' And do you know what? Her obsession began to take hold of me."

And, in a voice of voluptuous sadness, he said: "It's fatalism, old man. I leave the house every night with the certainty that I am going to my death, and when I clutch that woman to my chest, breathing in her breath, there are times when I shudder, feeling a stabbing pain like a dagger that pierces my heart. And I kiss her, kiss her on the mouth, on the eyes, on her hair—I give her my soul, my whole life. Crazy! I'm lost and I can't run away, I can't. This love is a destiny. It's stupid! Let's go."

He glanced around:

"And Brandt? One day he will explode at the bookkeeper. That fellow is savagely obnoxious and bad-mouthed to the point of infamy, with an irritating, viper nature. Brandt is right, let's go calm him down. He was mad when he left!"

The piano played softly and the light, filtering through the chalet window, gilded the glossy branches of the jasmine tree in bloom.

We walked on, and as we crossed the alley of the acacias, which was sweetly perfumed, I stopped the student from an imperious and urgent need to communicate my secret, to transmit to a subtle spirit the wonderful arcane confidence of which James Marian had made me the depositary.

"You said, speaking of James, that there must be a mystery in his life..."

"Yes, a divine mystery. I said it and I say it again because I feel it is so."

"You are right, Decio."

The student stared at me, squinting.

"Do you know something?"

"I know he's a poet."

"Yes, a hypostasis of Apollo."

"Or a madman."

"Why?"

"If he is not, indeed, a prodigy of Occult Science."

"I don't understand you, man. You speak a hieratic

language, you seem like an initiate announcing wonders."

"Must I?"

"If you promise to clarify these abstruse words, I tell you that even if I were in charge of shepherding the stars, the wolf Fenris could devour them because I'd prefer to listen to you and to your words, even sacrificing my love and the hours of this night with *her*, that promise to be stupendous. So speak!"

Suddenly, whirling on his heels and voluptuously inhaling the air, he boasted with rapture:

"The scent of magnolias! Flesh flowers, virgin breasts. Can you feel it? But speak up, tell me what you know."

Taking his arm, and at a leisurely pace, up and down the alley of acacia trees, I summarized in brief words the history of James' original text and the mysterious book itself, still barred to all sages.

Décio listened to me with a smile of incredulity and, when I finished the exposition, he burst out laughing with such pleasure that I myself couldn't contain my own laughter.

"You rode Pegasus, the dream horse. You dreamed a novel and you want to attribute it to the misanthrope. The process is known. Go, fetch the original text, you man of Fantasy, while I prepare the maestro's spirit, who is currently like the furious Ajax, to hear and enjoy your tale.

"I assure you, on my word, the truth of what I told you. I'll bring the original to convince you."

"Yes, man; go and don't delay. The night is beautiful. We will welcome the dawn to the sound of your punctuation, and the blonde goddess with rose cheeks will only have her pride. Go!"

And, laughing, he headed for the chalet, humming a fashionable tune.

The house looked deserted. The cold night had made the guests retire. In the basement, through the lighted windowpane, a slender shadow came and went. Crispim, of course, decorating texts. In the dining room, a gas burner gave little light.

I went up to my rooms and, clearing the desk, began to gather the strips, took the mysterious volume and was about to leave when there was a soft knock on the door.

Thinking it was Alfredo, who used to appear at night to review the room's arrangements, the pretext of which entitled him to a small gratification, I said, without turning around:

"Come in."

The door creaked slowly, there was a sound of footsteps and then silence. I turned around then, and great was my surprise to see James Marian before me.

I went forward to speak to him, with a sincere flutter of joy, but his cold withdrawal held back my expansiveness. I offered him my own work chair with stunned solicitude.

The Englishman looked like marble—eyes fixed, without the slightest ripple on his impassive white face, motionless and stiff, his hand resting on the back of the chair. He spoke in a paused tone and the words died before the last syllable, as if he lacked the breath to complete them.

"I have come to ask you for my writings," he said. "I must leave, I want to take them with me. If you have translated to the end, you know my singular life and the tragic story of an unfortunate man who drags himself painfully through pleasures in order to be dazed. If you didn't get the job done..."

"I have it almost finished. I'm only missing two pages that refer to your life in Brazil, if, in fact, you are the being in agony that struggles in such an extraordinary narrative."

"Yes, I am," he said, and turning pale as if in a faint, in a difficult voice he continued: "What you have not translated is little, almost nothing, and that little is worthless. My life in Brazil! Here I looked for Nature, I only related to the landscape and the light. I rested, and I miss the land and sky of that country of enchantment. Impressions... other than nature, I only have one left. The unfortunate woman who enslaved herself to my shadow gave it to me, who let herself be trapped in a dream... and died of love. I did to her what they say mermaids do to shipwrecked people: while they are warm, they hold them in their arms, but as soon as they die and get cold they reject them from their laps. I drank her feelings, I took them to my soul like sedatives, I lived on that love. A spiritual vampirism, perhaps."

"Miss Fanny?"

"Yes, her..."

"You *took* part of her?"

"Yes, and now I leave."

He lowered his gaze and his body swayed gently, his hair fluttering as in a hard gust. He buttoned up his coat.

"Where will you go? Please relieve my curiosity."

"I don't know. Give me the books."

I made a package of everything and, handing it to him, felt the icy coldness of his fingers. I wanted to shake his hand but he, withdrawing, made only a gesture with his head and, turning round, went slowly out as he had come in.

I followed him to the threshold of the stairs, watched him descend and disappear below. I heard his footsteps for a time.

There had been nothing extraordinary about that visit, yet I felt as if I was haunted, loosed in the void without stability and alone, very alone, abandoned as if the entire silent house had been emptied of its inhabitants and I was left behind to obsessive spirits that wandered vaguely through it. What could it be?! My flesh shivered in irritating twitches, my hair stiffened. I stood there for a moment, afraid, looking angrily, seeing tiny flames that ignited a funeral light and then disappeared.

I went back to my room, sat smoking, looking out the open window at the calm starry sky. "Why must that man leave?! What anguished haste would he have to hurry him out, as if fleeing with swift and silent steps?"

I shrugged, trying to get rid of the stubborn thought that haunted me like an obsession.

I thought I heard the door creak, click, open slowly, ever so slightly. I turned around quickly. Nothing, silence. Far away in the neighborhood, a piano sounded sadly, and the raucous horns of automobiles bleated in the distance.

Then I remembered that the student was waiting for me. I took the folder in which I had kept my translation and, remembering the incredulous words with which he had responded to my narration, I said to myself: "Of course you will laugh when I tell you that James has come for the manuscript and the mysterious book. In fact, just at the moment when I needed them to document what I had affirmed..."

But surely they saw him go by, leaving with the package. He wouldn't leave without saying goodbye to Miss Barkley...

And, no longer worrying about the incident, I went down to the chalet with my briefcase.

CHAPTER VIII

Décio dozed lazily, stretched out on the divan with his arms under his head, lightly swinging his crossed feet. From the bronze incense burner resting on the music stand, a slow, fine aroma of smoke drifted up. Sensing me, the student opened his eyes and stretched out his arms, sitting up and facing me, a smile unbuttoning his face:

"Did you bring the papyrus?"

"Somewhat. The owner took it just now."

"Who?" he exclaimed in a surprised yelp. "The Englishman?!"

"Yes."

"Did you see him?"

"For a short while."

"So that's why Miss Barkley sent for our Orpheus."

"Brandt?"

"That's where he is right now. Alfredo snatched him just as he was beginning a prelude by Dukas."

He threw himself heavily into the plush armchair and began to play with the tassels of an armband. Suddenly, in a rush, getting to his feet, he burst out laughing. "So the Englishman was worried about the mysterious book?"

"Well..."

"It's fantastic!" he exclaimed, laughing and squeezing me in his arms.

"You don't believe me?" I asked, embarrassed.

He lit a cigarette and said:

"Really, that type of man is one that impresses. If I had spent time with him like you, I guarantee I could have written a poem in rare verses, celebrating his beauty, grace and Olympic strength."

"But do you doubt what I tell you?"

"My dear sir, truth is beauty. What does the origin matter? You say it comes from that academic head, so be it! But you will allow all my praises to go to your modest genius. Sit down, open that folder and charm me."

"I swear to you that there is nothing here but the work of a translator and a bad one, and if I read these passages, which have little value in terms of conception and form, it is because I feel the mystery in them. For you, as for everyone who reads them, they will never go beyond pure fantasy, but I knew James intimately, listened to him, touched the scars on his body..."

"As Saint Thomas touched Christ's?"

"Don't joke. What need did this man have to present himself as a monster? Décio, his narrative was made with such painful sincerity that what struck me in it was not the wonder but the suffering. James Marian's life, if not a mystery, is madness wrapped in melancholy."

"Perhaps."

"Do you believe in the science of the Mahatmas?"

"I? In terms of science, I doubt everything. Mahatmas?"

"Yes, those solitary beings from India who preserve, like a mystical fire which will still shine in a new dawn, all the ancient wisdom."

"I know about that..."

"Well, my friend—either James is crazy or his life is an absurd paradox, the lie embodied in the Truth."

"Man, you speak with such conviction... What the hell! Is this serious?"

"On my honor, it is."

Decio got up worriedly, went to the back of the room with measured steps and paused contemplatively in front of the marble Venus de Milo, resplendent in the light. He fixed his enamored gaze on the white and divine body and said:

"This too is a mystery. All Beauty is mysterious. And by the way,"—he frequently improvised transitions that bewildered him— "do you know that I am anxiously looking for an Aphrodite, the perfect goddess, daughter of white foam?" He fell silent, eyes wide, ecstatic; and then continued sweetly, in slow words: "My old man, there is nothing better than water to preserve and give splendor to beauty. The bath, with a fine soap and a drop of scent, is a rite. The virtue of baptism is in the washing. There is no better perfume than that of water: the washed body exudes...." He paused and, ruffling his hair, exclaimed, "It's what delights that devilish woman—the scent of cleanliness. Because, I don't know if you've noticed—a washed body emits all the scents, like a garden... and water doesn't smell. White, not being color, is the fusion of colors, so water, being odorless, is the synthesis of aromas." He breathed in voluptuously and, with folded, adoring hands, praised the marine Venus: "Divine among the divine!" But soon, forgetting the goddess, he ran to the door, went out into the garden, and in the shade under the blossoming jasmine branches, muttered impatiently: "And Brandt, won't he come?" But almost at the same moment he exclaimed, throwing up his arms: "Here he comes!" Then, deepening his voice, he called out: "Hurry! We are waiting for you on the threshold of mystery. '*Speed up that thoughtful walk, enraptured man.*'"

And the artist replied in a smiling voice, calmly:

"Here I come."

The student advanced with light steps towards his friend and, taking his arm, asked him:

"What the hell did the Englishwoman want from you?" And then, suddenly jumping back, with severe respect and a growling voice: "Do you know that I'm beginning to distrust these nocturnal intimacies? Has the gentleman used incantations to unblock the monster's rigid heart?"

Brandt smiled.

"Miss is always the same virtuous and prudent Minerva, friend of peace and order. She called me to advise me, asking for a little more patience with the bookkeeper."

"Man, that is true... You were sparking today! Your eyes were like Zeus's, Olympus ignited in lightning. And so? Is the ribald one expelled?"

"I don't know... He's impertinent, perverse: he irritates me. Just listening to him makes my nerves tingle. He does not speak, but scratches and creaks. It's not anger I feel at him, it's frenzy. I'm afraid of myself."

"Do you want my advice? Break his face."

Brandt sat back on the divan, clenched his fingers and, smiling at me, asked:

"Is it true that you are master of the secret of James' life?"

"Yes, it's true."

"Wonders, huh? A poem that should be set to music by Debussy?"

"Perhaps."

He lazily stretched out his arm, took the pipe from the shelf, filled it with tobacco and said with regret: "I confess that I miss that man, and he left without a word, like a mute shadow. Miss Barkley only now learned of his departure."

"Departure?"

"Yes, on *The Avon*, the day before yesterday."

With a rush I sprang to my feet, electrified, feeling a tugging in all my nerves. My voice came out hissing, harsh, articulating the words with difficulty:

"Left! What? It's not possible."

"That's what I heard from Smith, at least, who's over there with Miss Barkley settling James' accounts."

Decio began to whistle softly, glancing about the room and, sensing my disturbance and so as not to embarrass me, he nonchalantly walked straight to the window and there let himself play with the jasmine branch.

"No! It's not possible!" I insisted. "You're mocking me."

"Ridicule?! I merely repeated what I heard," Brandt replied, unperturbed.

"I tell you, I tell you, it's not possible. James was with me about a quarter of an hour ago, up there. He came to get the volume he lent me, and the originals I translated. I spoke to him, followed him to the stairs..."

"You?"

"Yes, me."

We stared at each other in silence. Brandt, with his lively gaze, penetrating and clear, looked into my face and I, ashamed before the student, who was discreetly standing by the window, felt myself enveloped in a strange heat as if my whole body were slowly igniting. The blood was throbbing in my arteries, throbbing; my eyes were embers. Suddenly, a violent tremor shook me, a strong and immediate shadow darkened the room—or was my vision clouded-over in vertigo?—and when the light returned, I was at the piano, cold, shivering and twitching, and the two men, by my side, seemed to guard me, attentive and affectionate.

"What's wrong with you?" asked Decio, taking my pulse.

I answered in a frantic scream, insisting:

"It's just not possible! James was with me just a little while ago, he talked to me, he asked me for the book, the originals... It's not possible!"

Brandt was silent for a moment, eyes lowered, grooming his mustache. Finally, as if fearful, he said, in calm words:

"If you want to convince yourself... Smith must still be with Miss Barkley. Let's go there."

I threw myself out the door resolutely and into the garden, followed by the two men. I moved as if flying, without feeling the earth I was stepping on. The night air was frigid and I had the vague impression that I was sifting through fine mists.

At times, in a whirring vertigo, my head would rumble and seem to grow, dilate, or retract with a constricted sensation of squeezing, threatening to burst, and everything was unformed inside me—ideas swirled like a whirlwind, dry leaves in the gusts of a squall wind. I ran up the stairs.

Miss was talking on the porch with Smith. When they saw us, they fell silent. Brandt, calmer and forcing a laugh, apologized for interrupting the lecture to "rid ourselves of a stubborn thought" and asked the Englishman: "Is it not true that James has left on *the Avon*?"

"Yes, sir: he's gone. I left him on board."

As if thrown by brute force, I lunged at the Englishman:

"It's not possible!"

Such a sudden and violent denial made him turn around, scowling at me, and Miss, no doubt finding my bold objection strange, intervened, confirming the words of her compatriot:

"Well, he's left on *the Avon*. Didn't I see his name on the passenger list?"

I was stunned, and Brandt, in order to justify my attitude, explained to Smith: "He has assured us that James Marian had been, just a little earlier tonight, in his rooms."

"Oh!" said the Englishman, swaying in his chair. "James has eccentricities, surely, but showing up here when he's many miles out to sea, that—"

Miss smiled in agreement.

"And his luggage?" I asked.

"It was at my house, in Tijuca. The little he had here was taken, a few days ago, by my servant. I have orders to sell the furniture he acquired. The rest is from the house." And smiling, clapping his hands on his skinny thighs with a snap, he asked: "So... you saw him?"

"As I see you now, sir. What's more, I spoke to him, delivered a book he had lent me, and the originals of a novel."

"A book of scribbles and scrawls? I've seen that. It was always with him. In Java, it was stolen from him and he offered a thousand pounds to whoever would return it. It was returned to the hotel."

And Smith, as if such a short narration had fatigued him, let himself slide limply in the wicker chair, stretched out his legs, and, with his head down, his hands clasped on his belly, concluded: "time must walk on the heights of Bahia." He straightened up and, turning to Miss Barkley, picked up the thread of the lecture.

Brandt then took his leave: "Thanks! Goodnight."

He and Decio both went down. I stood, letting myself be, as if paralyzed.

"You're not coming?" asked the student, from the garden.

I made a vague gesture and took my time, looking around vaguely. Finally, slowly, limp, despiritualized, in a languor of brokenness, I walked towards the stairs and, without consciousness, climbed up.

Up there, out of breath, I took in long gulps of air, feeling a suffocating oppression. The floor slipped away from under my feet, the walls swayed, the ceiling vaulted, and the light, deathly livid and far from illuminating, was opaque, giving me the impression of a yellow wall that enclosed me—it was a light that immured, the funereal gleam of a tomb. Horrible!

Groping, I instinctively reached the door of my room. When I touched the handle of the latch, it was as if I had activated an electrical switch—the light brightened and shone helplessly: I saw! But my ears were like deep caverns that rumbled, a tempestuous roar thundered through my skull and, in a fervent hubbub like the rush of waves breaking on a rough beach, noises rang through me.

I threw myself on the divan, painfully squeezing, with icy hands, my stunned head. I could feel it growing, swelling, bulging like a balloon, and from all parts of the room, like ironic gravel, there came chuckles of mockery: it was a general mockery, the teasing of fearful things that unnerved me and retransmitted into a greater, unspeakable fear.

Oh! That fear!... It came like a flood. I felt it coming, rising, sensitive, palpable like the thick, dark waters of a flood. An itching of numbness tingled my feet, which were getting cold, freezing, like stone.

Fear reached my knees, girding me in heavy, intricate, constricted rings of iron, squeezing my belly, compressing my chest, and my heart began to beat frantically, very distressed as if forcing itself through the bars of the prison in an attempt to flee. My breath caught in my throat, the spasm tightened my jaws and, with gulps, it came as agonizing and rasping.

144

I stretched out on the divan, closed my eyes, and a ghostly vision flickered in the darkness: dancing puppets of fire, colubrine shapes streaked with lightning, a confused and extravagant juggling game of fire and blackness, sparks and tongues of flame in promiscuity with other bodies of indecisive shapes, now curved, now long; already spherical, already in turns.

I opened my eyes in amazement and suddenly, I leaned against the back of the divan, struggling to get up, but my energy was rendered useless in a flaccid, fluffy softness, as if I were stuck in a paste of cotton.

Out there, so close, life stirred! I could hear voices, the rumble of cars, the sounds of the piano; sometimes, in the breeze of the night, the sweet noise of the palm trees heaved like a panting of love. And I suffered.

As if it was turning off lights inside me, one by one, I felt the darkness advance, cold and tragic.

My brain darkened like a city at dawn. Long avenues were becoming shadowy, cloudy, deserted. I was going to pass away, it was my last day, my extreme hour and I was helpless, alone, without even the ability to call someone to my rescue because I didn't have a voice.

The eyes, powerfully attracted, turned towards the door, the door through which James, the specter man had entered and exited, and, looking at it, I saw that the whole wall dissolved into a starry background, which was the sky, while below stretched the railing of a ship against which, leaning motionless, eyes fixed on my face, was James Marian, handsome and pale, shrouded in mysterious moonlight.

Despite being dazed I still thought and reasoned, and I felt that I was the victim of a hallucination since the vision was perfect and clear as if it effectively represented the real. But no, this was my living room and, as I insisted on looking, little by little the visual faded, diluted; the wall reappeared, obscuring the sky, and the figure of the young man and where he was, the half-open door, faded out. Only then did I find myself sitting up, sweat beading on my forehead. I burned in the intense heat of fever, yet my teeth began to chatter.

In flashes and darkness, as in a storm filled by lightning, the voices of confused rumors echoed, vertigo returned and everything around me began to spin. I had the sensation of rising in the air, with the house, wildly, whisked away in a cyclone's driving force.

I stretched out my hands as if in search of support, got up in astonishment, even walked a few steps without balance, fell back against the table and, upon discovering my image in the mirror, my hair stood on end in terror.

I threw myself into spurred flight, but my movements were thwarted by a superior force and when I thought I had advanced, I found myself in the same place struggling, struggling uselessly.

I cried. Tears rolled from my eyes, thick and silent.

Words formed in my brain, came to my mouth and retreated without my being able to say them. The same cry darted and recoiled, like the ball thrown against a curb. It was horrible!

I was possessed, I was a victim of a succubus demon who infiltrated my soul with his spells.

He was a demon, a real demon. Oh! I felt it!

He'd been here. Moments before, I'd seen him, talked to him, given him objects, but he'd gone far away, across remote seas, unable to communicate materially with me. And how had he done it?

Sounds vibrated sweetly in the blessed silence, entered through the open window and gently visited my soul and then, as if because of their melodious prestige, the fearful noises that stunned me died away, thunderously falling silent, and I recognized Mendelssohn's *Wedding March*.

It was Brandt who played. It was he, the admirable artist who defended me with his divine art, who exorcised the obsessive spirit.

And for a moment—a soft and comforting moment!—I lay still, listening and thinking, in the solitude of that haunted room, so close to life and so close to death.

I concentrated on the music, as if I was in hiding. The sounds enveloped me, formed a true magic circle around me, and while the enchanting melody lasted, the fear, even though I felt it hovering around me, did not reach me. I was like a galley rower that had unfastened the shackle and laid down the chains—I felt the irons, but I did not feel the weight or the sharp, painful compression. Suddenly, however, the silence fell more muffled and soon the visions, the hallucinations began again. The terrible doubt reentered my spirit, torturing it. Was it possible for a man to manifest himself from afar, in a body real to the senses, in a living environment? Was it possible?

I got up suddenly and frantically, clumsily rummaging through the table with a nervous hand, in search of the mysterious book, the originals of the novel—and all I found was scribbled pages, quick jottings, letters, notes.

However, even that morning I had consulted the book. And all day, as if guessing the unforeseen outcome, I had worked without pause on the translation.

I stopped, tired and discouraged. My thoughts and ideas were confused, things from the past and my childhood, flowed in a mix with incidents of the day; reminiscences floated, emerging from the depths of memory in the violent revolving of my troubled spirit. My eyes, wide open and frantic, did not see the real, but instead bizarre chimeras: arabesques flashing in space, disks, streaks, flames dazzling in brightness or blinding in darkness.

A heat warmed me, gulfs of flame enveloped me, and then, in a sudden transition, the cold froze me, crippled me, stiffening me rigidly, as if I were locked in a prison of ice. I had a vague memory of fighting, figures swarming around me...

#

When I reentered life, what immediately struck me was the white room in which I found myself, almost as naked as a monk's cell. A man followed my steps attentively, dressed all in white, with an apron and cap. Promptly, he would respond quickly to my slightest gesture, he would sit by my iron bed, and at night I would feel him close, watchful. Sometimes, opening my eyes in the sad half-light, I saw him staring motionless, staring at me like an elfin creature.

Not infrequently, in the silence of the night, a voice shrieked piercingly: screams and wails thundered. I would shudder in terror, I would sit on the bed and soon the man would appear, reassuring me. He would start a conversation, or he would stay silent, smoking, looking at me.

Late one night, an agonized clamor arose throughout the place. I got out of bed, listening: "Where am I? What hospital is this?" I asked the guard who had come. He squirmed in a daze without finding a ready answer; he just said:

"You are already well. The director will release you."

The clamor ceased and the silence stretched out, muffled and more eerie.

Early the next morning, standing at the barred window of my room, I saw in the distance the luminous city, the blue sea and, below, at the bottom of the vegetable garden and park, men watering the fields and the sick walking slowly in the sweetness of the fresh air and through the carpet of the sun-shaded paths. But, from moment to moment, there came screams as if from a slave prison, the anguished and gloomy voice of those immured.

It was a hospital for the mad, for the mad! And I was there, observed by a doctor, watched by a nurse, followed everywhere, without freedom of movement, immediately surrounded like a dangerous beast if I deviated from the usual walk, taking the path uphill between hedges, which led to the monstrous body of the quarry which, from time to time, thunderously roared, shaking the place in earthquake-like oscillations? Just because of this?

One morning Decio appeared to me. Not as a cheerful and amusing companion, but as a restrained and discreet young man, speaking to me with a serene sweetness and thoughtful words, without the wild outbursts of his jolly temper.

It seemed he desired to probe my soul, before entering with his noisy and bubbling joy, fearing perhaps that it would awaken what was sleeping, or touch upon my frailties.

He was the only friend I saw in that sad room, he alone, no other, and it was with him and my correspondent that, on a radiant Sunday morning with the festival of the bells tolling, I left behind my prison cell and that man in white who, at times, seemed to emerge from the whitewashed walls like a bleached specter, walking towards me without soundless footsteps and his gaze hard and fixed and his hands tragically outstretched.

The correspondent, showing me a letter from my mother in which the unfortunate woman asked me to go to a farm accompanied by a person of trust, put himself at my disposal, declaring that we could, if I wished, leave that night. I agreed. As I gained the car, which was waiting for us at the door, and casting a last look at the formidable gate of the house where I had lived, unaware of the eclipse of my soul, I asked Décio:

"But then I've been crazy...?"

"Crazy?! What is madness, man!" He looked at me smiling and, as the car started, he grabbed me tightly in his arms and said to me with his vivid joy and all the warmth of his happy youth: "Neurasthenia, old man. Just neurasthenia! If you want to know, all of us without exception, if we were surprised at certain moments or in such "soulful states," would spend a few hours in places like this.

149

Don't think this is just for the crazy, it's also a shelter for those caught up in the passing storm of big dreams."

"And who doesn't have a screw loose?" said the correspondent.

"And my blast of madness was... James Marian?"

"Yes, the beautiful Englishman..."

"Was he a dream, then?"

"The existence of the man? No, he was seen. As for the incident of the book, his appearance that afternoon... do you remember?"

"Yes, I remember when he came to claim the book of his fate and the originals of what he intimated was the story of his own life. I remember. I was told such a visit was impossible because he was..."

"Many leagues at sea by then."

"Well, I assure you, I swear it..."

The correspondent cleared his throat, frowning at Décio. I reassured him by attesting to my perfect judgment and continued to the student: "If that's why they locked me up in that house, my dear Décio, I tell you that the alienists..."

But the student interrupted me loudly:

"Let's leave the past in the past. It was a crisis, a plunge into the deep blue. Oh, my friend, blue is only to be seen from afar, like this—"

And, bending down, he threw out his arm, in a sweeping gesture showing the clear, luminous sky, gleaming in the sun.

"A day for picnics," the correspondent stated.

"With women!" added the student.

And the car ran on.

#

I re-entered life like a convalescent who came out, for the first time, in the sun, feeling and enjoying all the charm of nature, participating in the general happiness, seeing the smiles and the sadness, passing between fortune and misery as if through two streets of the avenue of life. But the doubt, my God! The doubt which will be my eternal companion, the torturous doubt or, rather, the Certainty, which I will never prove to those who jettisoned me among the madmen, of the truth of that afternoon's incident. The horrible certainty of James Marian's visit, his presence in my room, his order, the delivery of the books and manuscripts, his departure, the sound of his footsteps on the stairs... everything, everything! This Certainty, my God!... But, Madness?

No, I am perfectly calm, I remember all the facts without omitting a single detail, I remember insignificant episodes... What do I remember most accurately?

And now, whoever sees me, will say I'm crazy. Those closing days made me useless forever... but I'm sure the Truth is within me: I saw it!

But who will believe my words? Who?

Perhaps the centuries will confirm what I say. The centuries!

When the day of Truth shines, who will remember a sad past?

Now I have my stigma, like a criminal sentence. I was in a madhouse.

So many innocent people have been judged... How many, like me, must have suffered for the truth? How many?!

Afterword

(Notes from the Translator)

As always, I note that I am neither a scholar nor an academic, and these are merely my observations.

I can honestly say that if any of the initial offerings from Strange Ports Press most exemplify my hopes for the ultimate purpose of this venture, it is Coelho Neto's **THE SPHINX** (*Esfinge*), from 1908. I truly hope this book will discover a new audience.

Here is a fascinating novel that touches on contemporary Occult tradition, through its interest in Symbolism (and "correspondences"), but whose ultimate aim seems outside the traditional realm of such texts – for in the conflicted and contradictory figure of James Marian, a masculine figure with a woman's gorgeous face, we find the true focus of the book.

Before we approach that, though, a word about some related aspects of the book. Obviously aesthetics, and specifically music, are an important part of the book's worldview. Frederico Brandt, piano teacher, music critic and expert composer is their main spokesman, articulating how music composition is the most spiritual, metaphysical, and direct of the Arts: "Music is an apparently easy language, but it is the most difficult of all. There are seven notes, some in the lines, as if thrown on the earth, others in space, hovering: reptiles and birds, carpet and cloud, flower and star. Seven are the values, seven the rests, seven the accidentals, seven the clefs, three the measures. It's little and it's everything. All voices, all noises fit on the agenda. The chords are five and enough: on them the subtle breeze hums and the fury of the storms rumbles loudly."

And further:

"If I consider music to be the most spiritual of the arts, it is because music is pure essence. Rhythm is its law, its manifestation is the sound of nature, light and ether, simple vibration, ethereal wave, nothing more. Music explains the invisible to me, in a way, and I understand the soul when I perform, I feel God when I compose... All artists descend from the ideal to the real, the musician ascends; from the real to the ideal. Poetry compresses Thought into words, sculpture is of stone or metal, architecture is mortar, painting is paint—music is rhythm and it is sound: the indefinite... Sound is like the smoke of censers—a winged prayer.

"In the temples, in primitive times, the lyres resounded near the censers and the waves, twinned, rose in the same flight—those of aroma, in cloud; the sonorous in melody. A poem is what it is—a stratification of ideas: the statue is a copy of life at a standstill; the building, a set of inflexible lines; painting is the vision of a point in space in the light of a rays of the sun. Singing is breath, soul, and, being soul, it is essence... Life is a rhythm that unfolds in rhythms as the wave multiplies in ripples."

Later, music serves to ease our narrator's suffering, even as it eased the soul of the dying Miss Fanny:

"Sounds vibrated sweetly in the blessed silence, entered through the open window and gently visited my soul and then, as if because of their melodious prestige, the fearful noises that stunned me died away, thunderously falling silent, and I recognized Mendelssohn's *Wedding March*... It was Brandt who played. It was he, the admirable artist who defended me with his divine art, who exorcised the obsessive spirit... And for a moment—a soft and comforting moment!—I lay still, listening and thinking, in the solitude of that haunted room, so close to life and so close to death... I concentrated on the music, as if I was in hiding."

But it is not simply music, but all the arts – as extensions of the senses – that contain the codes to appreciating the higher world.

From music, to perfume and scent:

"His fingers moved lightly, serenely, drawing from his soul that gentle *Pastoral* by Beethoven. The sounds were singing, spreading the divine poetry, opening the feeling to the mystery of nature, flying like dream butterflies into the dozing night, mingling with the perfume outside in the mystical serenity of sleeping space in the moonlight."

"Scent and sound, living in the air, insinuate themselves more than light: the frond of a tree is a barrier to the sun—scent and sound pass through the strong walls of prisons. In the brain, they are assiduous, and, visiting all the intricacies, they suggest ideas, awakening reminiscences, generating ecstasies and terrors, exciting jouissance or provoking tears. There are melodies and aromas that renew nostalgia, others make us daydream, winging us into full fantasy. A flowering garden inspires as much as an orchestra. And there are harsh sounds as there are aesthetic smells. The scent of the violet is a babble, the flowering jasmine is a bacchanalian chorus. The thyrsus of the Maenads, made of sandalwood, was said to be encrusted with gardenias and carnations."

To interior décor, furniture and sculpture:

"It lingered long enough for me to examine the richly and tastefully, if extravagantly, furnished room. A group of Louis XV, in yellow brocade, made up one of the corners, under the modesty of a clear screen flowered with lilacs. At the opposite angle was an oriental softness: on a Carmanian rug, limp cushions, concave stools, ottomans invited voluptuous stretches. Two wide ebony chairs carved in flowers and lace, with a back made by the open tail of a peacock whose plumage was exquisitely inlaid, offered in bloody damask the delight of open quilts which, yielding to the slightest pressure, warmed the children's velvet cushioned feet. And, in a gap, with satin pillows covered by a gold-colored strangle, magazines were scattered and still rolled in disarray on the white bearskin that was stretched out at his feet. Two pans on tripods gave off a vague aroma of incense. And naked, airy, on an onyx column, a flexible marble *bayadera*, her eyes half-closed, smiling, her bust curved, her firm breasts in the air, she arched her arms above her head playing a sistrum, her tiny foot badly planted on the ground, rehearsing the light step of a languid ballet. Two plinths stood tall and gilded, with *tremós* in wide frames in which curled little angel heads smiled between the leaves and in the center, under the bronze chandelier, the antique table, with twisted columns around which vast and fat burgundy Morocco armchairs opened up to the sensual softness of laps. There were flowers in profusion. They were forgotten in vases by the chairs, dying on the plinths, and one's feet pressed against loose petals, wilted bouquets, dried roses, all elastic as cloth."

To books and literature:

"The leaves, old, grimy parchment, crackled, creaked like tin sheets. On the frontispiece, two lilies clung to the same stem— one erect, in a starry bell, the other martyred, hanging in languor, and surmounted by a dripping heart pierced by an arrow. I turned the page and the text appeared in bizarre arabesques, with irregular shapes and complicated combinations: discs and sigmoids, wedge-shaped rods crossing or flanking Greek hemicycles in a descending shape, curved over the quivering line that, among the Egyptians, was the symbol of water, dots, chips, quotation marks and scrolls. Sometimes truncated profiles of men, animals, objects—a complex ideogram, a vast enigma of arcane or morbid fantasy."

Even the more recent (at the time) arts, like film ("a magic lantern with *delirium tremens*"), recordings, and photography, get considered:

"Then what is the phonograph? Is the cinematograph life in actuality, but the phonograph just all the mechanical chatter that whines and roars around, thundering through the city? Ah, but against this ignominy you do not rise up, why is that? For photography, my friends, has a guaranteed future. Everything will pass: the book, the newspapers, even the letters, understand? Even the speeches. All documents will be photographed... And politicians... will transmit their ideas through photography, showing there, on the screen, the advantage of their projects, finally exposing their programs live, not baiting the naive people with cute words."

Meanwhile, in the figure of Decio, we have an educated and literate man, but one whose view of the Arts is still caught up in the reductive and cynical allure of Decadence. His interest in Marian is simply of as a "strange being" and his assurance that the stranger's novel "must be original"— thus, merely the novelty of the figure and his writings excite him (just as in the novelty of his new, morbidly obsessed lover). As he expresses his jaded view to our narrator, after meeting in the dive bar:

"Then, dear sir, you are a sweetheart of the gods, the only man on this graying, exhausted planet who has yet been allowed to enjoy the super-excellence of a *thrill*. Because there are no more *thrills*. The few that remained, Baudelaire consumed. And you've found one! Happy man! And leave the superior feeling to splash in the slime of this infected, Suburran slum!"

But Brandt, and the text, argue that the Arts are not merely sources of *frisson*, but gateways whose contemplation can lead to higher realms.

At first, this manifests as lyrical expressions of the beauty of nature:

"After a light ablution, I dressed and, leaning out of the window, silently followed the farewells of the end of the day—the slow dissolution of colors, the religious silence of noises, the ecstatic recollection with which Nature makes her intimate evening prayer. I woke up when a sound, coming through space from afar, vibrated joyfully like a festive voice that woke me up. Stars were already shining."

"The waves, soft and languid, churned in spurts as in the wake of a ship. But the sky, behind the hills, was little by little serenely clearing as an eventual harbinger of dawn, a curved gleaming thread dropped below the horizon, the chains of the mountains shimmered with snowy light, and the enormous disk of the moon rose with the spectral impassivity of a vision, spreading on the waters its long silver path. A gulf of fire roared into the horizon. It cooled."

But then we are informed of Arhat's occult philosophy of correspondences (popular in occult lodges of the time, while originating in Baudelaire):

"Arhat used symbols as an expression of the mystery. What cannot be said or represented, is figured. Color is a symbol for the eyes, sound is a symbol for the ears, aroma is a symbol for the sense of smell, endurance is a symbol for touch. Life itself is a symbol. The truth, who knows it? The key of symbols would open the golden door of Science, of the true and only Science, which is the knowledge of the cause."

Which Brandt recapitulates, with his focus on music and the importance of learning to understand symbolism, and being open to what the arts have to teach us:

"However, as you began to be introduced to esoteric symbols, that is, to the 'intimate reason' of the ceremonial, your enlightened spirit would apprehend the beauty and significance of the most subtle passes and you would attain the ideal truth. Music is like that."

"It is not enough to hear it, it is necessary to understand it, feel it, interpret it: to have the emotion and the knowledge. In Beethoven's symphonies there is not an excessive note as there is not a useless leaf in the most verdant tree... All the harmonies of nature are contained within the fence of the pentagram."

"The music overwhelms me. Wagner was right—'it is literally the revelation of another world.'"

"Music, my friend, is a religion for those who feel it.... Bach's 'Prelude in E-flat Minor'. Worth all of Genesis, old man. Listen. It's all a creation."

But the Arts and the wisdom of how their symbols correspond to nature offer not only knowledge but succor from the pain of life, and ultimately the pain of death. Our narrator's harrowing vision of Death and sterilization, that follows the fumigation of the house, ends thusly:

"Then the torn-up skeleton began to move frantically, bobbing, gloating. She threw herself from the cliff onto the shroud and, stepping on it in triumph, danced and grew immeasurably, filling all the space until there was nothing left but the boneyard, overwhelming heaven and earth and, up there, where the ribs were like immense arches, was the huge, tabby skull, with two opaque eyes rolling in their sockets, like dead stars—corpses of the sun and moon, swaying and still illuminating in the last spasms... I awoke in agony, drenched in a sweat of suffering and, throwing myself out of bed, I stood in the middle of the room, terrified and appalled, and still the hideous smell wafted astringently, making the air thick and prickly.... The shadows of night were already melting, dissolving into the laughing colors of dawn. I went out into the sitting room and, receiving the healthy breath of morning full in my face, I breathed in long gulps, greedily, as if I had surfaced after a long, suffocating dive... I leaned out the window enjoying the wonderful apotheosis of dawn... The sky, with the various shades of dawn, from soft purple to the gold brocade, lit up resplendent nature as if an immense screen of fire was slowly rising, overlapping the soft, faint blue... The trees swayed in languid waves, their branches ruffled, and seemed to compose themselves brightly to receive the sun. The leaves, in the soft light that spread out in a swirl of gold, spread themselves with greedy eagerness... From among the leafy branches, all the gliding birds of France suddenly broke, and they were chirping merry trills and their flights crossed each other in an air show, as the sky, clearer, was warmed by the Sun that rose in triumph."

And through symbolism, Brandt argues Man is capable of understanding Death and his own place in the scheme of things:

"I judge Death to be an ascension, nothing more—what we

call Life is the purification of being. Nature, that's all. The soul enters into existence as on a scale of perfection, it passes from the smallest to the greatest, oscillating between good and evil. In every man there remains a vague reminiscence of a previous life and there is a tendency towards the beyond: the earth holds us, the sky attracts us. The victory of the Absolute is Death... We were a tree, trying made us a bird, instead of captivating roots we acquired the loose wing, to win space. Man today, tomorrow..."

And this ultimate understanding is achieved through poetry:

"Poetry is the flower of Truth, my friend... The poet is a seer: he announces by symbols what is to be accomplished in the days to come. The flower has no earth, only aroma: the verse is pure abstraction—soul. The fruit, with the tasty pulp, comes later to the tree. Analyze any scientific law and you will find the poetic essence in it. The first sages were contemplatives: the word of Wisdom was born to the sound of lyres. Apollo guided the footsteps of infant Minerva. Everything is poetry."

Which makes Miss Fanny's rather rote and mechanical burial service seem abhorrent:

"No! I do not understand religion without ritual, nor ritual without pomp. Man needs to *see* in order to understand and love. It is not enough to think of God, it is necessary to feel him, to have him before the eyes in material expression, as a target to which the prayer goes, to which the begging hands are thrown and the unleashed tears run in torrents... All this is creation, not God. And this chapel is a deserted house, a dead body that is missing... The soul, old man, the soul of religions, which is precisely Poetry: an expression of Goodness, Love, Hope, Faith... the symbol, the symbol, the eternal and necessary symbol."

"Consider a barge to the port, rig the boatman to sail, secure the oars, remove the rudder, tie it up and jump ashore. In the heaving wave, the boat continues to hum. If the cable that holds it tight breaks, it moves away, crashes or capsizes, but if it doesn't break the line and escape the shelter, it stays until the owner returns, who climbs on the deck again and heads for the open sea... Life is the sea, the boat is the body, the boatman is the soul."

All of which, once we learn James Marian's secrets, might makes us wonder at his origins as a "creation" of Arhat, and what he/she (they) may ultimately symbolize. For, as Decio says: "Imagine, the most beautiful head of a woman on the formidable torso of a circus Hercules. Beauty and strength. All Aesthetics!"

And it is obviously the figure of James Marian that is the main focus of, and interest in, this novel. Because they can be seen as both a person and as a symbol. As a person, they receive some of the friction and vituperation one might expect of a figure of contradictory gender in a work from 1908 – and yet Neto obviously intends us to see in Marian something more than simply a target for abuse or a figure of pity (although on this later point, the author still has to deal with the expectations of cultural mores and limits on expression of the time).

His initial description illustrates the contradiction:

"But what immediately surprised, by contrast, in this magnificent athlete was a face of soft and feminine beauty. The limpid forehead, serene and flowered with gold by the rings of hair that rolled gracefully across it, the wide eyes of a thin and sad blue, the straight nose, the small, red mouth, the plump and white neck like a vine, blooming the head of Venus on the massive shoulders of Mars."

Unsurprisingly, the sarcastic Basilio tags Marian as a "sissy" and notes that he always "classified him in the other sex," demanding "well, is that a man's face?!" But then, Basilio seems to have no ability to read beyond the surface appearance of things, and so Marian's contradictory visage is probably confusing and frightening to him – "Basilio lashed out, indignantly, against James' beauty, with the scandalized revolt of a Puritan in the face of obscene turpitude." Note also that, much earlier, Decio defines the landlady, Miss Barkley, as "a man crippled in a woman."

Miss Fanny, as we discover, is romantically attracted to Marian (although her later succumbing to consumption ends that romance) but the real question remains – is our male narrator also enamored of the (ostensibly) male Marian?

Again, while it would be unlikely for this to be directly addressed at the time and place this book was written, there are any number of hints. He find's Marian's "handsome face" to be "charming." Their first interactions are described in the language of a budding romance:

"He took my arm and I, increasingly bewildered, trembling as if I were being dragged by an assassin into a back alley, far from all help, was intimately enchanted by the proposal that left me on the threshold of the arcane, binding me, by intelligence, to that strange man, whose beauty was a mystery, greater, perhaps, than his eccentricities."

"He stopped, transfigured, his mouth half-open, looking at me with his big sad eyes, and after a moment he said in a vague, subtle tone, as if in love's confidence:

"'It's... my... novella.'

"A shiver ran down my spine. In a deaf and trembling voice I asked:

"'It must be pretty!'

"He blushed, shrugged his shoulders, pursed his lips, and, as if for air, shook his head, which shone like gold, anxiously in the sun."

"Then, catching me by the arm, he snuggled up to me, casting a pallid look around. I could feel his panting and the rapid beating of his heart."

And the narrator himself even comes as close as he can to expressing it directly:

"He put his arm around my shoulders. A fine aroma wafted from his body, and his breath, which washed over my face, was warm and aromatic. Caressing me with a lover's blandishments, he led me to the terrace and there, among the plants, in the open air, we sat down... Again he took my hands—his were freezing cold—and looked at me closely, with the terrifying eyes of someone trying to extort a secret. But sweetly, a smile broke out on his face... A smile... why should I alter my impression?... enamored. And then I had the certainty, the painful, poignant certainty that the soul of that man, which shone in beauty, was... what to say?"

But more than that, we find that Marian himself leads a conflicted existence over their own status as Arhat's creation.

"It was not love that surrounded me, but care. I was his workmanship, the work of his knowledge. He had great zeal for me, always attentive to my health, to my sorrows, medicating me, defending me from all evil so that I could resist. I was to him like a delicate object kept in a display case. There was no love. What has he done for me? He gave me life, educated me and made me heir to the fortune I squander. I was sleeping and he woke me up... and now I'm sleepy, just wanting to get back to sleep."

Even Arhat, his spiritual "father," a Mahatma of great metaphysical abilities and wisdom, who saved the lives of two children by melding them into one, seems unable to see a happy future for the individual he has "created." He attempts to let "nature" decide (with the introduction of Maya and Siva into their household) but is left to state after this fails:

"If the feminine predominates in you, which shines through in the beauty of your face, the face of your sister, you will be monstrous. If you conquer the spirit of man, as the vigor of your muscles would have you believe, you will be like a magnet of lust. But unhappy you will be, as there has been no other in the world, if the two souls that hovered over the revived flesh managed to both insinuate themselves into it.... Woe to you if the two principles manage to penetrate you—discord will walk with you as the shadow follows the body. Loving, you will be jealous and disgusted with yourself. You will be an incoherent anomaly: wanting with your heart and hating with your head, and vice versa. Your right hand will declare war on the sinister one, one of your cheeks will be on fire with shame and disgust, while the other will be inflamed with the modesty that is the flowering of desire. You will live between two bitter enemies. There! That is you... Tell me, where does your heart take you? What do your senses claim? Where do your misty dreamlike eyes linger more charmingly?"

Which is really no help at all, which Marian finds as he further embarks on his problem-filled journey through life (such as his first experience of love, in Stockholm). It is with this background knowledge that the choice of "Sphinx" as a symbolic term for Marian really resonates – the head of a woman on the body of a lion, representing Wisdom and the Bestial, while also posing as the keeper of great Secrets and Riddles.

There is so much more left to unpack in this fascinating novel—which it would be glib and reductionist to sum up as a "gay/transgender **FRANKENSTEIN** narrative" (as much as that may hit some of the high points). But I thought I might leave you with this.

Marian obviously feels his existence and interactions with others are cursed, which we can understand given that, of the two people who deal with him closely/have visions of him, Miss Fanny and the narrator, one dies of consumption (which Marian attributes, perhaps unfairly, to a kind of "emotional vampirism" on his part) and the other is driven mad for a short time.

But I note that another character, Brandt, also has a vision of Marian and does not suffer, and so I ask if it is a coincidence that the composer has the most advanced understanding of the interpretations and uses of Symbolism? Note that earlier he says "Love is a fixed idea: it rises from the heart in feeling and becomes thought in the brain"—which touches on Marian's exact circumstances (being the heart of a man with the brain of a woman).

And further, I note that one of Arhat's last proclamations was: "*If you manage to discover a privileged intelligence that interprets symbols, you will be in the world like an angel among men, lord of all graces, of all prestige, a sovereign will in a wonderful spirit.*"

So perhaps we should not read Marian's situation "realistically," but "symbolically"—and see hope for a brighter future.

STRANGE PORTS PRESS

(strangeportspress.weebly.com)

Offering you the finest of previously unavailable stories and novels of the strange and weird from the world over, newly translated into English and with an afterword by the translator. Check out our website for the following offerings, as well as upcoming titles!

STRANGE TALES

MALEVOLENT TALES (Cuentos Malévolos) (1904) by Clemente Palma

Dark and twisted stories of decadence, horror and the supernatural (along with a few bitter fairy tales) from Peru's forgotten master of the macabre! Contains the notorious story "The White Farm," and 18 others!

MALIGNANT STORIES (Historietas Malignas) (1925) by Clemente Palma

Another selection of Palma's decadent pieces, augmented by 15 previously uncollected stories! Includes the shocking novella MORS EX VITA, as well as meetings with the Devil, a near surrealist expedition into the sewers, and a Kafkaesque bureaucratic nightmare. A total of 19 pieces are offered here.

STRANGE NOVELS

THE BLACK MAGICIAN (Der Schwarze Magier) (1924) by Paul Madsack

A strange occult terror novel concerning The Master, a popular sculptor (and "influencer" of his day), who uses his powers of dark sorcery to expand his influence (and profit), even as he attempts to bring the unsuspecting, small-town painter Fiedler under his sway. A far-ranging novel, this includes glimpses of the political and cultural realities of Germany at the time, as background for a supernatural stew of weird scenarios and visionary excess.

THE SPHINX (Esfinge) (1908) by Coelho Neto

A strange mixture of Symbolist and Occult Novel, concerning a boarding house in Rio de Janeiro who react to their mysterious fellow boarder, Englishman James Marian, who possesses a virile masculine body but the beautiful features of a woman. Our narrator agrees to translate a strange text for Marian, one which reveals his complicated and metaphysical origins, even as tragedy strikes the small compliment of friends and associates. An intriguing, if abstracted, meditation on gender and love, this novel by the Brazilian author deserves a larger audience.

THE VAMPIRE (El Vampiro) (1910) by Froylán Turcios

One of this Honduran writer's oddest works, this is a Romantic/Gothic novel with overtones of Decadence. The idyllic life of young Rogerio Mendoza and his beautiful cousin Luz are disrupted not just by a predatory priest, but by a legacy of violence and mysterious death in his family line. Those seeking a Honduran version of DRACULA should seek elsewhere, but this intoxicating and beautiful tragedy casts a strange spell all its own. Includes an Afterword by the Translator.

Made in the USA
Las Vegas, NV
26 December 2024

15378801R00098